DAWN'S DESTINY

ROMANCE ON THE OREGON TRAIL BOOK 3

KATHLEEN BALL

I dedicate this one to my Granddaughter Clara. It's her birthday today and from the moment I held her she took a big piece of my heart.
I also dedicate this to Bruce, Steven, Colt, Clara and Mavis because I love them.

CHAPTER ONE

*J*oyful melodies from fiddles, concertina, and harmonica drifted on the night air. Muted laughter and soft conversations joined with the song. The music played on, though more and more people were heading toward their wagons. Mothers ushered children, gentlemen escorted ladies, perhaps in hope of stealing a kiss.

Independence Rock towered over them, and Heath realized just how tiny humans were in comparison. His replacement for guard duty should be arriving soon. He knew they had opened a jug of whiskey before he'd taken up his post. Would there be any left?

The thought of the amber liquid took him back to Ireland, to the days before the Great Hunger. There always was whiskey aplenty but as soon as the potatoes rotted for the second time, no one had a coin to pay for such a luxury.

He sighed. America was a great country but he missed his homeland. He had saved what he could and then he and his brother Declan made the horrendous trip to Boston Harbor. They weren't afraid of hard work and had become popular at the docks for being reliable workers. But they'd longed for more. They wanted what they couldn't have in Ireland. They wanted to own their land.

The sounds of merrymaking were left behind as he drew near the wagons. He nodded to one of the other men on the wagon train with them and headed out toward the livestock. He, Declan, and their friend Zander had hired on with Harrison Walsh as drovers. They took care of his twenty head of cattle and impressive string of horses.

He heard a grunt and peered in the direction it had come from. An Indian stood up and stared at him. What was Eagle Nest doing here? Was he following the wagon train? Heath had his hand on his pistol in its holster as he walked toward the tall man.

"Eagle Nest," Heath said as he nodded. He waited to see what the Indian wanted. At one point in their journey Eagle Nest had wanted his now sister-in-law, Luella for his wife. It didn't happen, and Eagle Nest had been a good chap about it.

"Lu-ella. I need Lu-ella. I have white girl here and she needs to get away from Kills Many."

Heath glanced at the girl with Swift Eagle and had to keep himself from openly cringing. She was filthy from head to toe. She wore a doe skin dress that had several rips in it, and it looked as though someone had beaten her face.

Heath nodded. "I'll get Luella and Declan." He walked back, keeping to a leisurely stroll and trying to act in a normal manner so as not to draw attention to himself. He arrived at their wagon to find they had not yet retired for the evening.

They looked cozy sitting next to each other, talking in low voices, and holding hands. Whatever Declan said to Luella made her face turn red.

Declan looked at him and frowned. "We were just about—

ouch." He looked at his wife in surprise after she elbowed him in the side.

"What your brother means is we were thinking about going to sleep."

"Eagle Nest is here, and he has a hurt white girl with him and he wants to see *you*, Luella."

"Swift Eagle? I told you before his name is not Eagle Nest. Show me where he is," Luella said as she stood up.

"I'm coming too." Declan stood right beside her.

She nodded at her husband and as Heath set off for where he had left the Indian, they followed.

Eagle Nest—or Swift Eagle, he supposed—stepped from behind a bush, startling Heath.

Luella smiled. "It's good to see you again Swift Eagle."

"It is good to see you too." He gestured behind him. "Sunset is hurt. Can you fix her?"

Luella gasped and stepped forward, taking a closer look at the woman accompanying the Indian.

"What do you mean by fix? You want me to tend to her so you can—oh dear... Where did you get her? I know you didn't do this to her."

"Kills Many beat her and he wants to kill her in a bad way. She said no. Will not be wife."

"Swift Eagle, will Kills Many come looking for her?" Heath asked.

"He thinks he killed her when he threw her off a cliff, but she lives. Lu-ella, you are a brave woman of my heart. I know you will help."

Luella nodded as she took the woman into her arms, almost falling from the weight of her.

Heath swept her up into his arms, and she whimpered.

Luella hurried and hugged Swift Eagle. "I'm honored you brought her to me." She pulled back and smiled. "Will I see you again my friend?"

"I go to my tribe and make sure Kills Many believes she is dead. You always in my heart Lu-ella." He turned and walked away into the darkness.

"Bring her to our wagon," Declan instructed in a brusque tone.

Heath nodded, already heading in that direction. The girl was in such distress and was obviously struggling to stay quiet. He carried her with ease; she weighed little more than a child. Her face was swollen and bruised. Her lip was split, and the blood had dried. Swift Eagle had claimed she was white... He peered into her face, but he couldn't tell. She looked like an Indian to him.

The light from the fire didn't show him much more. Whatever she had put in her hair smelled putrid. He set her on the wagon tailgate keeping her in his arms so she wouldn't slip to the ground. Declan put quilts down on the wooden floor of the wagon and set out all they had to use for injuries and sickness.

Declan jumped down and lifted Luella up into the wagon. "I'll heat the water," he told her and hastened away.

Heath gently laid the woman down and left the wagon. She'd probably feel better if there weren't any men in there.

He glanced around, but most folks had already retired. No one was paying them any mind save one man named Eddie, who stood watching them, his expression openly hostile. Eddie wasn't the nicest of men. Heath gave him a quick nod, hoping the other man would turn away but he sat by his fire and stared in their direction. Nothing stayed a secret long on this journey. When he saw Captain London hurrying over, Heath groaned.

"I heard there's an Indian in the wagon," the older man said in disbelief.

"She's white and hurt. You remember the Indian Luella's Pa tried to sell her to? He brought the woman for Luella to take care of. I think she was a captive." Heath said. He hated being outside of the wagon. He wanted to know what was going on.

"How hurt is she? Was it that Eagle Nest fella? Has he been following us? Did you see any other Indians?" He fired the questions off without giving Heath time to respond. Then he waved an agitated hand through the air. "We'd best double the guard."

"He was alone. He was trying to get the woman to safety and away from the tribe. He left as soon as she was in my arms. He thinks a lot of Luella."

The captain relaxed his shoulders and nodded. "To be safe we'll double the guards. I'll just tell you how it is with female captives. Other females don't want to be tainted by them. They all claim they would have killed themselves rather than live with Indians. It'll be a hard road for the poor gal. You get permission from Harrison to have her in his wagon and it's fine by me that she travel with us."

"Thanks Captain."

"Everyone will know before the sun is up." He tilted his head in Eddie's direction.

Heath nodded. "The same thing occurred to me. I'll protect her."

Captain London gave Heath a long look before he nodded. "I'll leave her in your capable hands."

Heath watched him leave. Then he hurried and poured the heated water into a basin for Luella. "How is she?"

"Her injuries will heal. It's her mind I'm worried about, but maybe it's too soon. She's terrified, even of me. She was tortured." She took the offered basin and went back to the girl.

Heath sat next to Declan who had just come back with more wood for the fire. "Have you ever seen the likes?"

Declan nodded his head. "People coming out of English

prisons. The women especially were broken shells of who they'd been. Some were able to heal but they were never the same. The inhumane treatment, the vermin and the shame was too much for some. I've seen people walk away from their families never to be heard of again. I heard one woman say the best thing to do was to let them be. Allow them to make the decision if they want to talk about it or not and don't push them to do anything. I suspect this is much the same, well, probably worse."

"Did you know that Eagle Nest is really Swift Eagle?"

Declan laughed. "Of course I knew. Do you think Luella would allow me to call him by the wrong name? He gave her an eagle feather, you know, which is a great honor. Feathers are earned, not just given. My wife is quite a woman."

"You were fortunate, indeed, on that. You both looked happy tonight."

"We have finally decided that we will build a future together—with you and Zander of course. Where is Zander?"

Heath shrugged his shoulders. "I saw him earlier and he mentioned one of the Turney girls."

"Which one? There's the oldest, Mona, then Jane and the youngest Cindy. But the oldest can't be more than fifteen years old. He'd best be respectful and keep his hands to himself." Declan shook his head.

"Speak of the devil," Heath remarked, and then he chuckled. "Looks like he's limping."

Zander sat by the fire, heated anger emanating from him. "That Eagle Nest is on my list of people who need to be taught a lesson. He clocked me from behind and then he tied me up. I finally got loose and expected to see you all dead."

"He brought an injured girl to Luella. I guess he didn't have time to explain it to you," Declan said.

Heath nodded. "If he hadn't wanted you to be able to

untie yourself he would have tied you tighter. And his name is Swift Eagle."

"He didn't bring any of his tribe with him?"

"No, he just dropped off a white girl," Declan said, shaking his head. "Luella is tending to her now, but it'll be a long road for the poor lass."

"I thought you were supposed to kill yourself if Indians caught you. I've heard that advice often. What kind of future will she have? Not a good one I can tell you that," Zander spouted.

"Think about it, Zander," Heath said with a flash of irritation. "First, it is against our religion to commit suicide but if it wasn't and you were captured would you just kill yourself? We've survived more than most, and my life will not be taken by my own hand. Plus I'm thinking they won't be providing you with the means to kill yourself. We're not able to talk to those who did kill themselves to know if they regret their decision"

Declan laughed. "No, they aren't, are they?"

Declan stood and lifted his wife down from the wagon. "How's she feeling?"

She put the dirty cloths and towels into the washtub and poured the rest of the hot water on them. Then she filled the pot again and put more water on to heat. She sat and sighed. "She doesn't have any broken bones. She had enough cuts that I need to see if I can find some comfrey in the morning. She's asleep, but I'm going to make willow bark tea for the pain. There are new bruises on top of old bruises and there are probably older ones under those. Her name is Dawn. From what I can gather her family lived in a settlement. They were attacked, and she and six others were taken. Her baby and husband were killed. She has no one. I bet once the swelling goes down she'll be very lovely." Luella met Declan's gaze and something unspoken passed between them. "No male is to approach her. I'll talk to Cora, and I think between the two of us we'll heal her wounds, but she's trembling and can't seem to stop. I'd appreciate it if everyone showed her kindness even when talking about her." She glanced left and frowned. "Eddie's been watching us? I'm hoping everyone on the train will treat her with the respect she deserves but I've heard what people say, and it'll get ugly."

She sighed and poured herself a cup of coffee. "Zander, are you all right?"

"Your Indian beau clocked me and tied me up."

"At least he didn't kill you." She sat down. "I'm going to take a break and then get breakfast going."

"We can cook for ourselves," Declan told her. "I'll help you rinse out those clothes and then I'm tucking you in for a few hours of sleep. Cora will be up soon. She'd probably be happy to help."

DAWN'S EYELIDS FLUTTERED, but only one cracked open to let in a bit of light. Her other eye was swollen shut. She needed to stay awake. Who knew what these strangers would do to her? The woman seemed nice. Luella, what a pretty name. There was compassion in her eyes, not the horror Dawn had expected.

She must be a frightening sight to all the white people. Her body ached from the beating and the fall. The ride here hadn't helped, but Swift Eagle was very kind and very gentle. He seemed anxious to see his friend Luella. And he had been right to want to see her. There was kindness in her. A kindness for which Dawn was truly grateful.

Had Luella cringed when she'd seen Dawn's body? It was marked, scarred, and burned. The Lakota Indians had entertained themselves watching Kills Many torture her. Her heart hurt for those she'd lost and never had a chance to mourn. Almost every moment of her time with the Lakota she was kept busy. Perhaps that had been just as well, since thinking about what happened at the settlement where she had lived was too atrocious.

There had been times when she thought she'd lose her mind completely. It happened to captives; they couldn't deal with what happened and then they weren't right in the head. Eventually they became too much trouble and they were killed.

She'd had to encase her heart to preserve her sanity. There had been a few white people who acclimated to the way of life of the Sioux. The children were mostly adopted by families. The adults' fate was always something that could change at any time. She'd been given to Kills Many's wife, Dancing Girl.

Another woman climbed into the wagon and Dawn began to shake. Her breaths came in short gasps as emotions threatened to overwhelm her. She needed to concentrate on what was happening now.

"I'm Cora, Dawn," she said in a soft tone. "Luella and I are friends. I came to see to your wounds. I have an ointment I made from comfrey."

Dawn nodded, unable to speak past the fear swelling in her throat.

"Good, you know of it. I know you had willow bark tea but I do have laudanum if you need it."

"No! I'll not be drugged so you can leave me behind." There were two ways out of the wagon, and if she had to she'd use one.

"We have no intention of leaving you anywhere. Is there someone we can notify that you've been found?" Cora's voice was lilting and gentle. She didn't hide her feeling behind a mask as many did.

"I have no one. Everyone is dead. I doubt anyone ever looked for me. I had hoped at first—" Her voice cracked and she took a moment to catch her breath. "But hope faded eventually."

"I'm sorry." Cora hesitated, seeming a bit awkward. "I'm going to have to take your dress off so we can put the ointment on. Tell me, are you hurt worse on your back or your front?"

"Both. I don't think anything is broken." She winced as she shifted and spikes of pain punched through her chest. "I think I have a cracked rib, and I'm bruised pretty bad. I have more open wounds on my back."

"Is it all right if I cut your dress off of you?"

Dawn's throat tightened. "Are you planning to use a knife?"

"I have scissors in my basket," Cora hastened to assure. "I'll cut it right up the middle from the bottom to the top. After that, I'm going to make sure the rest of you is clean. Luella did a fine job but it's hard to see everything with just a lantern. Then I'm going to treat your wounds, and finally I have a nightgown you can put on. I don't think you'll need to leave the wagon for at least today. You need rest."

Dawn nodded and tensed her body, waiting for the woman to get the scissors. What if Cora attempted to stab her? No one could be trusted. It had been a lesson she'd learned the hard way. She kept her eyes on the shiny shears and was ready to spring up if need be. How agonizing it was. It seemed to take forever for Cora to cut the dress.

Cora put the scissors back in her basket, and Dawn relaxed a bit and helped get the dress off. It had been slightly used but clean and serviceable when she'd been given it. Now it was stained, ripped, and filthy. Some of the doe skin stuck to her back, and Cora spoke through the opening in the wagon's back, asking someone to bring her water. The dress was soaked off, and when Dawn saw all the blood on it, her stomach churned. She was lucky to be alive.

Cora kept Dawn covered except for the area she was working on. It was such a courtesy that Dawn's good eye grew moist. There hadn't been any privacy for her in a long time.

"Am I hurting you too badly? I'm trying to be gentle, but I have to clean your wounds. Did they burn you?"

She nodded. "They put sticks in the fire and when the tip caught fire they took it, blew out the fire most of the time and then put the stick on my skin. Most of the time I didn't scream; they respect a person who is strong. I'm not strong, though. I just wanted to stay alive."

Cora's eyes widened.

"I shouldn't tell you all of this. I would have been very happy not to know a thing about the Lakota." Her gaze wandered to the rear of the wagon. She could hear muted voices just on the other side of the canvas. "Those men outside won't come in, will they?"

"No, you are safe," Cora said. "My husband, Harrison Walsh, owns this wagon, and Luella and Declan use it as their own. Declan, Heath, and Zander are men my husband hired to drive his livestock across to Oregon. They are respectful and kind men. They've all been through their own tragedies. They would never harm a woman."

"I don't feel very trusting." Oh, how she wished she could control her shaking voice.

"I don't blame you."

Dawn hissed as Cora washed burns in sensitive areas. She closed her eyes and did what she always did lately.

Lord, I don't know how to thank You. I'm away from Kills Many, but You know that. You were with me and I know You guided Swift Eagle in finding me. I don't know anything about these strangers, and I'm afraid. I've been afraid since the first cry I heard on that awful day. I don't know what I'm supposed to do. I have faith.

"I need to turn you onto your stomach."

Dawn nodded and turned over. It was a position that was hard to fight from. She wished she had her knife but Kills Many had taken it. Deep breath after deep breath didn't calm her. Her muscles refused to relax. Being so tense made the pain worse.

CHAPTER TWO

"*G*o back to the wagon, Heath!" Declan yelled from a top of a paint. "You'll end up hurt. Go make sure she's all right."

Heath wanted to speak in denial, but he didn't want to lie. He slid off the horse he'd been riding, and Declan took the reins.

"Cora and Luella could probably use some help," Declan said before he left with both horses.

True they probably needed water hauled, and he knew the women were making more than the normal amount of bread while they had an extra day at Independence Rock. Many were washing clothes too. There were other things he could do besides bake and wash.

The sun was beating down on him but there was a nice breeze. Anything was better than the sand they'd been traveling through. He looked at the Sweetwater River and longed to dive in. Perhaps later he'd have a chance.

There wasn't anyone outside of the wagon and he glanced inside. Cora was tending Dawn's back. He quickly looked away. It must have been worse than anything living with those people. Would she act like one of them? Even before Zander had mentioned it, Heath had heard a woman was better off dead than to live with the Indians. That she was no longer respectable or allowed in polite company. If that was truly the case, what a shame for the poor girl.

Cora started to climb down from the wagon, and Heath hurried over and helped her down.

"Well what do you think?"

"Think?" Cora snapped. "She's been through such evilness; I think she's a strong survivor." She gave him a strange look. "She is hurt and it looks as though she hasn't eaten a full meal in years. She was tortured and beaten, and I can't imagine coming through such a thing. I haven't heard most of the details, nor will I ask her. If she wants to talk about it then I'd be happy to listen, but it's her business."

"I think it's all of our business," Della, the good Minister Paul's wife remarked. "I brought a Bible for her. She needs to renounce the devil."

A crowd had started to gather and gasps hissed through the throng as many of them nodded.

"I do believe it is by the sheer will of God that she is here. We don't need any salacious details. She is here to heal and decide what she wants to do after that. If I hear one word against that poor girl you'll have me to answer to," Cora said in a loud, strong voice.

Heath stood shoulder to shoulder with Cora portraying a united front. Cora's threat that anyone would have to deal with her was a bit laughable seeing as she was almost too nice. He glowered at the crowd, hoping they got the message that they would have to go through him as well. Most turned and left except for a few of the women.

"You'll need to keep her away from the others for her own safety," said Sue Bandor, Cora's friend.

"We'll protect her," he declared.

"I know you will," Sue Bandor assured him.

Della handed the Bible to Cora. "Can you give this to her and let her know both the minister and I are here for her? No questions asked. I'm sorry for what I started out here. I should have thought before I spoke. My first words should have been 'how can I help?'"

Cora took the Bible and hugged Della. "None of us have been in this situation before. We are forever learning."

Della beamed as she left.

"If that's a taste of how people are going to act, we're not going to be very popular around here," Heath said.

"I never was. I need to get back to Essie. I'm sure Luella will be up soon."

"I'll just sit right here." As he watched her walk away, panicked thoughts flooded his head. Could they really leave her with him? He couldn't think of a thing he could do to help her. Maybe she wouldn't need anything. Maybe she's sleeping. Should he go and wake Luella? He sat and tried to stay still. A groan of pure misery came from inside the wagon. He was familiar with that sound. He'd heard it often from the starving and dying people in Ireland.

Before he knew what he was doing, he'd climbed into the wagon.

She took one look and put her hands out in front of her as if to defend herself and almost screamed. It looked as though she swallowed her scream instead.

"Ah, lass, I'm sorry I scared you. I'll leave, I just heard your pain and wanted to lessen it."

She sighed, which he took as a good sign, and then she put her hands at her sides on top of the blanket.

"Would you like some water?"

"Luella said there is willow bark tea?"

He smiled. "You're in luck. I actually know how to make it. I don't know if you remember, but I carried you to the wagon last night. I'll get your tea." Heath climbed back out. Hopefully, one of the women would be by and could take the tea into the wagon.

As he prepared to brew the tea, he considered what he had made out of Dawn's appearance. It was going to take a while before all the swelling went down. Her hair looked lighter, but he wasn't sure. She smelled a lot better.

Luella stepped out from the tent and smiled at him. "Where's Cora?"

"She had Essie to feed. Dawn would like some willow bark tea. I was just about to make some more."

"That's nice of you. Tell you what. I'll make the tea if you'll hunt up more firewood and make sure the water barrel is filled."

"Firewood and water, I can do that." Heath walked a ways to find wood. Seeing the Turney girls, Mona, Jane, and Cindy took him by surprise. All three turned crimson when they saw him.

"Being careful out here I hope?" he asked.

"We're just talking," Mona explained.

"Actually you can probably answer a few questions for us," Jane said as she stood. She put her hand on her hip and tilted her head giving him some type of smile.

It took him a minute but he realized she was trying to look like an appealing woman. She was fine without the pretense.

"Does she bite?" Jane asked.

His eyes opened wide. "What? Do you mean Dawn? No, she does not bite. Where'd you get an idea like that?"

Cindy jumped up. "It's well known that she is nothing but a wild animal and shouldn't be around people. You do have her tied up, don't you?"

"Where did you hear all this? And no, she's not tied up."

"There have been meetings. Everyone is talking about her," Mona explained.

"I, for one, side with the majority. We want her left behind," Jane said with a firm nod.

"Then it's a good thing that Captain London is in charge. It could happen to you, you know. You're here in the woods without protection. It's not a good idea, especially since an Indian brought Dawn to us. They're in the area. She was captured and hurt. She needs our help. Aren't we supposed to help each other out, or is that just on Sundays?"

Lorelei's jaw dropped. "You're one to lecture. I don't think I've seen you at any Sunday service this whole trip."

"I have wood to gather. Have a serious thought to your safety." He stalked away from them, picking up wood as he went. It was going to be a tough fight to keep Dawn with them, even though most were good folks. People were just scared of what they didn't know.

Lord, You know I don't go to Sunday services. I guard the camp instead. I figure we're on good terms. I ask for Your help in tolerance and patience and anything else I need, to not punch anyone. You led Dawn to us, and we will take care of her. I know it won't be easy but we can do it with Your help.

With an armload of wood he walked back to the wagon. He tensed when he saw the crowd that had gathered. Pushing his way through he set the wood down and put a few pieces on the fire. "Did you get a chance to make the tea?" he asked Luella, ignoring the rest.

"Yes, she's drinking it now. Her wounds are looking better." She glanced at the people closing in around them. "I don't like this many people crowding in on us."

No, he didn't either. "Folks, it's time for you to go back to your wagons," he called out. "We would appreciate some privacy."

"Heath, we have a right to know if the little heathen is

17

going to slit our throats in the dark of night. She might be some sort of spy for the Indians," Davis Bird said.

Heath had thought Davis to be a nice enough man, but now... "This is not the place to show your displeasure. Captain London is in charge."

"I have some chains we could put her in!" one man shouted.

"Chained outside for us all to see. She needs to be guarded. She might try to run. Who knows what she learned living with the Indians?"

"I won't feel safe until she's gone!"

"I say we make the rules and leave the captain out of it!"

Heath put his hand on his gun. It was like some kind of mutiny. Luella scrambled into the wagon and came back out with a shotgun. She pointed it in the air and shot. Without saying a word, she just leaned against the wagon.

It wasn't but a few minutes before Declan, Zander, Harrison, and Captain London rode to the wagon.

"Make way!" the captain shouted. "What's going on here?"

"Sounds like mutiny to me, but with Luella on our side I'm not worried," Heath said.

"We want the prisoner chained up outside with an armed guard. When we leave tomorrow we want her gone," Davis Bird explained.

The men immediately got off their horses and stood next to one another creating a solid line in front of the wagon.

Captain London scanned the crowd, and many glanced away. "Luella, you've spent time with Dawn. Has she harmed you?"

"No, she's a gentle soul."

"It's all for show," Davis Bird insisted.

"She didn't harm me when I talked to her," Heath said. "In fact she's afraid of us, and I'm sure your hostility isn't helping. Without going into any detail, she has many wounds that need tending. I'd say that she had a very hard time."

Captain London stood on a crate. "There will be no mutiny. There will be no chaining or tying up the young lady. There will be no guard, and we will not leave her behind. We are her people and we need to take care of her. She was not captured by any fault of hers, and praise the Lord she was strong enough live through her ordeal. Now if anyone is interested in making a dress or knitting some socks or a shawl for her, let me know. I'll see what I can rustle up for you. Meeting over." He stepped down his face disgruntled.

"You've got a good head on your shoulders, Heath. Can't really say that I've seen this side of you before."

Heath's face heated. "I've always had my brother. We didn't know a soul when we came to America. I can't imagine doing it myself. Besides, everyone needs a helping hand don't you think?"

The captain smiled and gave Heath a slap on the back before he went on his way. The heat didn't subside. Heath was very aware of Declan's and the other two men's perusal.

"I'll sleep under the wagon tonight," Heath said before he left. He laughed to himself knowing they probably stood there with their mouths hanging open. There was no shame in helping another.

DAWN STARED at the wagon canvas as she listened. That one man had been very nice to her, but could she trust him? No. No, the only one she could trust was herself, and at times she wasn't so sure of that. She couldn't always trust herself to be strong at all times.

She'd grown up in a settlement and married the man of

her dreams, her best friend since they were toddlers. Their daughter, Patricia had been born almost nine months to the day after their wedding. She'd been the sweetest girl. She hadn't had much hair but what she did have was a blond color. Her father, Lincoln had doted on her. Dawn and Lincoln hadn't been married a year before Lincoln was shot dead and then Patricia was killed a few hours later.

Dawn squeezed her eyes shut trying to keep out the memory of her sweet child's death. No matter what happened over the last months it couldn't compare to what they did to her innocent baby.

Pushing up the long sleeve of the soft nightgown she wore, she studied her arm. It was covered in knife wounds and burns. Some were older than others just as some were deeper than others. She'd endured and survived. There had been many times she wondered why she kept going? There was no one waiting for her. It had been almost unbearable to hear a baby cry. She often talked to God and He was her only link to sanity.

Now she was here.

Lord, I hope this is the path You have chosen for me. People don't want me here, but there is a family, actually two families that act as though they are willing to protect me. Bless Swift Eagle for bringing me here. I have no doubt this will be hard, it already is. I wish I could trust, but I just can't.

Luella crawled into the wagon and smiled. "I have a Bible for you. It's a gift from the preacher's wife, Della. If you don't want it or don't believe, that's fine."

Dawn took the Bible and held it to her chest. "I will treasure this. I don't belong anywhere, do I?"

Luella blinked in surprise. "Why do you say that?"

"I heard the people outside." Dawn couldn't quite meet Luella's eyes. "The Lakota didn't really want me, and now my own people don't want me either. It was hard to hear. I belonged to Kills Many's wife . She didn't believe in sparing the rod or asking me to do something first. She always had a switch nearby. I wasn't the only one she hit. She took great joy in hurting Kills Many's sister. I guess some people have meanness in them. When Swift Eagle found me that was the first time in months that I hadn't been hit and burned."

"I'm so sorry, Dawn. It must have been hard to bear it. You are a strong woman. We want to give you time to heal and we'll take it from there. Don't you worry. There is enough food. We'll start off with a small bit of food so you don't get sick. I'm going to make flapjacks with bacon. I can make you something else. Cornmeal mush might sit better."

"I'd like a bit of bacon with a flapjack. Food was either bountiful or there was none. They didn't save or ration. They ate until the food was gone and their stomachs were over filled and many did get sick. I was never given enough to be full." A sigh slipped past her lips. "I know I'm an inconvenience, and I'm sorry."

Luella put her hands on Dawn's arm. "Don't be sorry at all. I'll get busy making breakfast. I'm sorry Heath was in here."

"There is gentleness inside of him. I don't think he even knows," Dawn said.

Luella smiled and crawled to the back of the wagon. A man with big strong arms lifted her down. Was that her husband? Dawn sighed. Lincoln was very much like that. She could hardly remember his voice and it scared her. She'd have to live on the memories of their days together for the rest of her life.

HEATH SAT LONGER at the fire than he usually did. The sun had gone down a bit ago, and Luella and Declan had retired to the tent. They'd been giving each other long looks and big smiles while at the campfire, so Heath was just as glad when they left him.

He'd been assured by Cora that Dawn was sleeping. Dawn read the Bible for hours. He never once heard her complain or ask for anything. He had helped to hang extra blankets for privacy when the women bathed. Dawn took hers first, and he thought he heard her laugh, a light and uplifting sound.

There was something about her...but he couldn't figure what it was. He wasn't one to bring home hurt animals or people. He thought maybe he was just concerned for her, but that wasn't like him. He usually was drawn to women who were robust and not as thin. He banked the fire and laid out his bedroll under the wagon. Then he quietly rolled beneath the wagon and closed his eyes. He sure was tired.

He woke suddenly without realizing why and grabbed his gun, glancing in all directions to see who was around the wagon. But he didn't see anyone. He listened for the sounds of footsteps but heard none. A moaning of pain reached him from inside the wagon. Someone must have gotten in there. He rolled out from his bed and stood with his gun still drawn. He stopped at the back of the wagon. The pain-filled noises grew louder. The canvas was still tied closed, so he quietly untied it and loosened the cinching so he could get in.

It was now silent except for the chirping of grasshoppers. He put one leg over the closed tailgate and then the other. Then he was wacked on the side of the head. He saw stars floating in front of his eyes. He gritted his teeth against the pain and tackled the man.

Once he had the man pinned, he realized it wasn't a man. "Dawn?"

"I'm going to cut out your tongue and then burn your eyeballs. After that I'll take one hand off and then the other.

Get off me." Her voice was low and entirely serious. It gave him a chill down his spine.

"Dawn, It's me Heath. I do tend to talk too much, but no one had ever threatened to cut out my tongue before." Still in his hold, her body relaxed.

"Get off me please." Her voice shook.

Heath rolled off her. There wasn't much room in the wagon and his shoulders still touched hers. He turned to his side and looked down at her. It was almost pitch black in the wagon, and it took a minute for his eyes to adjust.

"I was sleeping under the wagon, and I heard groaning. I thought someone was hurting you."

"I woke when you untied the cinch. I grabbed a log of wood and hit you hard. Oh my, are you all right?"

He touched the side of his head and grimaced. "I saw stars for sure. It's a bit tender. I'm just glad I didn't pull the trigger."

Her mouth formed an O. "I'm sorry I woke you. I didn't think I made noise anymore. I used to cry all the time, but if I woke anyone, I was whacked. I doubt I'll ever be a normal person again."

"You've probably been through hades," murmured Heath. "I can't even imagine. Now we know I'm a light sleeper."

"I don't know, I can be loud. Oh, what if I woke others?"

"Don't worry I didn't see anyone when I jumped in here. I'll just say goodnight then."

"You don't think anyone in the wagons will try to harm me, do you?" Her body tensed.

"No, besides they know one of us sleeps under the wagon. You're safe."

"One of us? I'd like to know who is under the wagon."

"Fair enough. Tonight it's me. Sometimes it will be Zander, and if we both have guard duty Declan will. Sometimes we switch in the middle of the night if the shifts run that way. We'll keep you informed each day." He inched to the back of the wagon. "Can you cinch this?"

She nodded.

"Goodnight."

As he dropped to the ground, two shadows slid deeper into the darkness, but he didn't see who it was. He walked in that direction but found no one there. Shrugging, he returned to the wagon and rolled back under it.

It took some time for sleep to come. Dawn's fresh scent lingered in his memory. He thought her hair might have been lighter than the brown it was now, but he wasn't sure. It had been dark. There was something about her that drew him. Sighing, he closed his eyes.

CHAPTER THREE

Once she gathered her strength, she would walk. This jolting and bumping in the wagon was painful. Dawn sighed. She didn't want to leave the safety of the wagon and the other people on the train didn't want to see her. When she'd left for brief moments, eyes had widened and she saw a few men hover their hands over their guns.

She also wasn't used to doing nothing. The Lakota had kept her busy every minute. She hardly had time to think about anything except for finishing the task she was given quickly and efficiently. Any delay was met with the switch against her, and Dancing Girl didn't particularly care where she struck Dawn. Kills Many got upset only once, when her face was bruised.

As Dancing Girl's slave, she had to have permission to do anything. If Dancing Girl decided not to feed her that day, Dawn went hungry. She'd slept outside the dwelling on many cold nights. It had been a hard life until Kills Many decided to take a liking to her. None of the other women were happy about it and burning her with fire sticks became their favorite thing to do.

Dawn's thoughts drifted back to the present as she sat at the back of the wagon so she could see out. They passed a woman with her infant. Longing and loss filled her, and she let the tears fall. If she closed her eyes, she could clearly see Patricia being killed over and over. Her grief had never lessened for Patricia or Lincoln. There were many times she wished it had all been some horrible dream. Who could imagine such cruelties? How she'd endured, she hadn't a clue.

Glancing at her hands she wondered if her skin would ever stop peeling. The sun hadn't been a friend to her. She'd been horribly burned over and over as she was in the sun all day every day. Dancing Girl had laughed when she asked for a hat.

And now... it seemed everyone expected her to take a bit of time and then be normal. She didn't know how to be normal anymore—or what normal even was. It wasn't just a misfortune; most of her had died when her family was killed, and the rest of her had been beaten until she was afraid of her own shadow. She did learn how to keep her emotions tucked away. She always stood straight and tall no matter what. It wouldn't have been a good idea to allow them to know she was shaking on the inside.

And now... She couldn't just sit in the wagon. She had done nothing to be shamed for. There was work aplenty, and she could be of help. Maybe it would be easier to find sleep if she worked hard. But it was unsettling to have a man sleeping under her, even though she was aware that it made her safer from the others.

The sun had shifted and soon they would stop. She had a pretty green dress that Cora had given her, and she'd also given her a bonnet. It was a poke bonnet that wasn't attractive but it kept the sun off her face and she treasured it. She even had shoes now.

Declan was driving, and he slowed the oxen and took

their place in the circle of the wagons. He was a very nice man who treated Luella grandly. They were so in love it hurt to watch them. When the wagon stopped she lowered the tailgate and climbed out.

They would need plenty of buffalo chips. She hadn't seen a tree all day though they weren't very far from a river. She could smell the water.

"You can stay in the wagon if you rather," Declan said kindly.

"Do I have to? I'd rather resume some activity."

He smiled, a warm expression that showed in his eyes. "Whatever you feel up to. It's good to see you on your feet. I know Luella enjoys your company."

She smiled at him, and it felt strange on her lips. "You're lucky to have each other."

"I have plenty buffalo chips!" Luella's eyes sparkled.

Declan's lips twitched. "If I had known you'd be so happy about the chips I'd have given you them to you."

Luella shook her head and put the chips next to where the fire would be lit. "How are you, Dawn? It's good to see you up. Declan, could you get her a crate to sit on?"

"I would like to help today. I feel useless, and it's not a good feeling."

Luella nodded. "There was a bit of luck. The men hunting have enough elk for everyone."

Dawn nodded. "That is a blessing. It will help me regain my strength. I'll start the fire." She was sore from being in the wagon. It was uncomfortable moving about so much, but it would help her and she'd get stronger every day.

She set the tripod over the fire and put a big pot with water hanging from it. "What's next?"

Before Luella had a chance to answer one of the drovers dropped a bit of elk at Dawn's feet and then he threw the skin at her. "You can make yourself some new clothes." He laughed as he rode off.

Blood from the skin splattered all over Dawn. She stood very still and then picked up the meat and washed it off. "There's a river a mile or so from here. Could you get me the other dress you gave me? I'll put it on after I wash."

Luella looked as though she wanted to cry. She went into the wagon and carried out clothes, a flannel towel, and some soap. "You shouldn't go by yourself."

"I know how to take care of myself. Thank you." Carrying the bundle, Dawn set out walking. She could feel people watching her, and she shook inside, but her knife, Swift Eagle had given her, was hidden in her stockings and she knew how to use it. It took a while of walking, but the water was there to greet her. Her heart lightened a bit. After glancing around, she undressed and got into the river with the soap.

It felt wonderful to be alone, and the river, though a bit strong, was refreshing. She was strong enough to stand against the current. She washed her dress and washed her body, taking delight in using the soap. But it was getting late, and she needed to walk back. She wrung out her dress and threw it near her clean clothes then climbed the bank, grabbed the towel, and began to dry herself.

Thundering hooves had her glancing up, startled. A horse and rider were headed her way. She didn't dare drop her towel to dress, so she grabbed her knife and stood in the slight breeze waiting. Her body tensed, and all of her senses were heightened. She'd been a good pupil when watching the Lakota practice fighting, and she was exceptional with the knife.

She breathed a bit easier when she recognized Heath, but she kept her stance widened, ready if she needed to be. Her towel threatened to fall, and she quickly tucked it around her again.

"Hello, Heath. Out for a ride?" She kept her eyes on his face. She'd already noted his sidearm and rifle.

"Truthfully, Miss Dawn, I was sent to find you. Luella is positive you were either captured or dead. I guess you've been gone longer than she thought you'd be."

A bit of guilt pricked her conscience. "I didn't mean to worry her. The river was a bit farther than I thought and the water was delightful. It's been a while since I've had soap." She pushed a smile onto her face. "A man might not understand."

"I do understand. I'll turn around while you dress, lass." He slide off the horse and held the reins as he stared in the direction of where the camp was.

His chivalry touched her. He'd make some woman a good husband.

"You do know it's not safe to be here alone, don't you?" he said.

"I'm fine. I'm very exacting with my knife. Learning to use it was hard. I usually ended up hard on my back. But the Lakota learn how to protect themselves when they are young."

"If they let you have a knife, why didn't you stab and run?"

"Where would I run?" A wry chuckle slipped out. "I wouldn't have gotten anywhere before I was grabbed and tortured. If I was lucky they'd kill me."

"That's a good reason. Luella told me what happened and I'm sorry it happened to you."

She finished dressing. "I'm clothed. I suppose it will be my life now. People will think me more Indian than white. It's fine. At the end of the road I'm going to get some of that free land and grow everything I need. I'll keep to myself, and I should be fine."

He stared at her.

"What's wrong?"

"You have blond hair," he murmured. "I'd wondered…" He shook his head. "And you're too faired skinned to be outside for long."

"Sometimes you don't get the luxury to sit in the shade."

He walked closer to her. "Very true, and I know how much it can hurt. I'm sorry I'm staring. I've talked to you but usually in the evening. You are beautiful."

She bowed her head. Then she stood straight and tall. "Get on with you. I'll be right behind you." She picked up her things and bundled them in the towel. Then she started to walk. She didn't want to be beautiful. She just wanted to be unremarkable. It would be bliss to walk anywhere and not be noticed. She glanced up to heaven. *You can't change, what's done is done.*

"Dawn?"

"Sorry, I was wool gathering I suppose. Was there something you wanted?"

"I wanted to know if you wanted to ride the horse."

"It's a kind thing that you asked me, and I thank you. But I've found this walk to be very calming. There is no one but you and me out here. I can be unafraid—for the moment at least. I can pretend that all is well." Tears stung her eyes. "Once I get back to the wagons I'll be reminded that I have lived with the Sioux. I never learned to give the look of disdain that many in the party seem to have practiced repeatedly. I act as though I don't hear them or see them but it chips away at my dignity every time. That's all I have left. I put it on like a great cape, and I just hope it's not so tattered and torn that it will be useless. I suppose I could always try to sew it back together, but I don't think it an easy thing."

"Doesn't it get weary?"

"I suppose it does. It's like trying to struggle upstream in a very strong current. You get knocked down. If you don't get back up you'll either drown or be pushed downstream, and sometimes downstream is worse than where you're at. But there are times in life that there is nothing you can do to change fate. What happened simply happened, and it can't be undone. I've railed at God so many times, but I've also praised Him. I've learned to try to live by the words I read in the Bible. The problem is the others. I can't control anything."

Heath made a noncommittal grunt.

It was nice to have him walking at her side instead of in front of her. She glanced at the horse. It was a fine dun he was leading. It would have been a good mount for the Lakota to steal.

He twisted his head and gazed at her. "The wagons are in sight, and I see your shoulders growing tense."

"Yes, I need to stand straight and tall with my dignity wrapped around me and the tensing of my shoulders helps." She smiled at him and then touched her lips. "I'm not used to smiling anymore. I've missed it. Will you stay with me until we get to the wagon? I've run the gauntlet once and that is enough for a lifetime."

"Of course I will. Would you like me to punch the man who threw the bloody skin at you?" He raised his brow.

"No, revenge is better when it is unexpected. I've been taught many things but have never put them into practice. I believe some will find what happened to be funny and others will disapprove of it. With the Lakota, it would have been my job to clean and soften the skin. It's hard work."

"I don't know about you but I'm hungry."

Heath kept talking as they walked to their wagon, telling her silly stories about life on the wagon train. She knew he was deliberately telling her of the lighter things, there had been without doubt many troubles and tests had happened along the Oregon Trail, but he kept such dark tales to himself. He was a good man with a big heart.

HEATH COULDN'T KEEP his gaze off Dawn. He tried, and he tried hard. They were all seated around the fire eating dried apple cobbler.

"I heard you folks had some trouble," Captain London said as he strode over to them. Luella quickly grabbed another crate for him to sit on.

"Can I tempt you with some cobbler, Captain?"

"I must confess I could smell it and it made my poor old full stomach rumble."

Everyone laughed.

"I've had a talk with Chuck Klass, and he won't bother you again, Miss Dawn."

"Thank you." She looked very uncomfortable.

"How'd you find out who it was?" Heath asked.

"Luella gave me a description, and the lout was standing near the livestock bragging to some of the others. I just happen to be standing behind him. He's been given extra guard duty. I wish I could have done more, but you can't do much just because someone is meaner than a rattlesnake." He dug into the cobbler Luella handed him. "This is good. My compliments, Luella."

Declan put his arm around his wife. "I got lucky to marry such a wonderful wife."

Everyone agreed, and Luella turned crimson.

There was a pause in the conversation. Then London spoke up. "I'd appreciate it if you all keep an eye out for

Dawn here. People aren't always as tolerant as I would like. Dawn, please don't go anywhere alone."

The flare of irritation in her eyes was gone so fast, Heath was sure he was the only one to catch it.

"Of course, Captain. Thank you for your consideration. I don't plan to spend my days in the wagon anymore. I'll stay close to it though."

He finished eating and nodded. "I'm glad to hear it. We'll be at a trading post in a few weeks. We can leave word that you've been found."

"Thank you." Her eyes locked with Heath's. She had a serene appearance, but he knew she was hurting. She had no one who was looking for her.

The captain stood and tipped his hat to the two women. "Thank you for the wonderful food and delightful conversation." He made his way to the next wagon.

"He's right," Declan said. "We need to keep our eyes out. I know we've been traveling with these people for months, but some I just don't know if they can be trusted. We can rule out any of the married men. Their wives wouldn't be so easy to forgive such a thing no matter how they personally felt."

"We've been sleeping under the wagon," Zander said.

"I know and thank you. I can take a turn if you have somewhere else you wanted to sleep," Declan said with a teasing smile on his face.

"I'll have to let you know. I haven't had any invitations from the ladies yet." Zander laughed. "I don't mind. I did want to ask you one thing, Dawn. If you're having a nightmare would you want to be woken? I haven't known what to do some nights."

"I'm sorry I disturbed your sleep. Heath told me I groan in pain when I sleep. I'm just surprised by the whole thing. Such things as nightmares or noise at night were reasons to be switched. I don't want to disturb others, so I suppose waking me would be the best. But don't touch me. I don't want to stab you by mistake."

"You sleep with a knife?" Zander didn't sound very happy.

"Yes. If you'd lived my life you would too. I am free, and I will fight to stay that way. I'm sorry you're upset, Zander. You can leave me be if it's easier." Her expression was blank and Heath wondered what she really felt.

"I'll be here most of the night," Heath said. "I'm sure we'll get it all worked out. Unless someone complains I wouldn't worry about the noise. You're just loud enough to alert us something is wrong but we've slept like that for a long time, ready to defend ourselves in an instant. We don't sleep through much." He watched as his brother and Zander nodded solemnly.

Harrison, Cora, and their baby Essie stopped by to visit. Dawn couldn't seem to keep her gaze off of Essie. Cora must have noticed too because she put Essie in Dawn's arms.

Dawn seemed to be in her own world, talking to the baby and smiling. Her eyes had a haunted look in them.

"You're good with her," Cora remarked.

"I had a daughter. She was about the same age as Essie." Dawn stood and handed the baby back to Cora. Then Dawn stood at the edge if the firelight and looked out at the dark emptiness.

"I didn't know she had a child. Where is she?" Cora whispered.

"Maybe she had to leave the baby behind when Swift Eagle brought her here. But I can't imagine she wouldn't have been planning to go get her back," Declan said.

"She's spoken to me some…about her life. I'll go talk to her," Heath said. "Clean the dishes and then make yourselves scarce."

They all nodded, and then Heath walked slowly to Dawn.

He stood at her side and it took her a while before she acknowledged him.

"Her name was Patricia, and she was born exactly nine months after I was married. Her hair was blond and her eyes were blue. She'd grasp my finger and, oh my, she was strong. I thought I had it all, a fine husband, a beautiful baby, and a beautiful house on rich land. I don't remember a time when I'd been as happy." She swallowed hard and was quiet for a few moments.

"Lincoln, my husband was just coming in from cutting wheat when the Indians rode in on their horses yelling. I went into the house and grabbed the rifle. I put Patricia on the bed and by the time I got to the door they were slitting my husband's throat. I tried to close the door but it was too late. They were in the house. I pushed one aside, Kills Many, to get to my daughter but he just backhanded me."

"They tied my hands behind me and pulled me out of the house. They shoved me to the ground. I tried to get back up but Kills Many slapped me again and down I went. He carried Patricia out and I thought for sure he'd give the baby to me. She cried and cried. He held her by her feet and slammed— She was dead. I was broken, but I refused to cry in front of them. They ransacked the house and took so much."

"I couldn't watch my things being taken out of the fine house Lincoln had built, so I stared at a clover patch in front of me. I actually found a four-leafed one. There was a chill in the air and I shivered. Kills Many brought out my shawl and put it around me. I secretly hoped they'd kill me too. But that wasn't the plan."

"Kills Many retied my hands in front of me and threw me up on his horse and then he vaulted up behind me. They started the house burning and it was then that I saw smoke behind the house. They'd already been to at least to three of my neighbors' homes."

"We rode into the woods where there were more Indians watching the prisoners. I was pushed off the horse and hit the ground hard, but I didn't make a sound. I think by then I was numb."

Heath put his arm around her. "Let's go sit by the fire. It looks like everyone wanted to give us some privacy." Gently, he turned her and walked her to a crate where he helped her to sit. Then he settled onto a seat next to her and took her small hand in hers. He could feel her pain but she didn't cry and her voice never cracked like some did when telling a sad story.

"I'm so sorry about your husband and baby," he said, keeping his voice soft.

She blinked at him and then nodded. "They were what kept me going. I know revenge isn't very Christian but I thought about it all the time. I even made many plans of how I would do it."

"If seeing Essie is too much—"

"No. I enjoyed having a baby in my arms again. I'm sure after this journey is over I won't get a chance. I was never one for big dreams. I was content to live in the settlement. I'd known Lincoln since I was a toddler and when Patricia came I felt complete. I'll need to find something I'm good at. Something I can get paid for. It's been a long day, Heath."

"I'm tired too." He stood and pulled her along by the hand. He led her to the tailgate and put his hands around her waist then lifted her into the wagon. "You hardly weigh a thing." She smelled so clean and fresh. "Please keep your snoring as quiet as you can. It sounds like nothing I've ever heard before." He smiled.

"I think scratching the wagon floor would make an interesting noise. Don't you agree?" Her eyes twinkled as she returned his smile.

He laughed and shook his head. "Good night."

Dawn pulled the cinches nice and tight. Then she put everything she'd need for bed next to the straw tick. She'd have to dress in the dark. Her lantern would cast too many shadows and she didn't need anyone looking at her. She blew out the candle and made quick work of getting ready and into bed.

Her mind began to whirl with memories of Lincoln and Patricia. She'd had many content days with hope for the future when they were alive. It was still hard to think of them as forever gone. Heath was becoming a trusted friend but that was all he could be. No one would marry her after she'd lived in an Indian village.

She closed her eyes and fell asleep.

CHAPTER FOUR

*H*eath repeatedly turned his head trying to see Dawn. She insisted on walking. Thankfully, she wasn't alone for long. Cora and Luella both walked with her. Dawn even took a turn and carried Essie for a while. The wagons ahead of him slowed and came to a stop. It was time for the nooning.

He jumped down to the ground and watched Dawn come to the wagon with Luella. Was Dawn limping? Had she twisted her ankle?

She gave him a lopsided smile as the two women stopped at the wagon.

"Did you fall?"

She looked down at her skirt. "No, why?"

"You're limping. It looks as though you're in pain."

"There wasn't a choice in clothing or shoes. I'm fine, really."

Understanding rippled through him. She hadn't arrived with shoes on. Her feet must be a mess. That was a problem he would have to think a bit on. He headed off with Declan to find Zander and check on the livestock.

"She's very nice when you get to know her. She wears a blank expression a lot but not with you," Declan said.

"I was able to get her to trust me. We talk a bit. I feel bad for her."

"When's the wedding?"

Heath's jaw dropped open. "Never. I'm not looking for a marriage formed because of necessity. I want a woman who loves me."

"I got lucky with Luella. I can see the love she has for me in her eyes. I never thought I'd be happy again." Declan smiled.

"I had my doubts about you too. I thought she'd ruined our dreams with new dreams that the two of you had. And it shames me that there was a twinge of jealousy. It's always been you and me. We do have a future to build, and I'm looking forward to the challenge. Just think we'll be land owners." Heath couldn't even believe he was saying the word *landholder*.

"I never thought we'd see a day when that happened. Do you ever remember Ma and Pa being happy? Before the Famine?" Declan asked.

"They certainly didn't make eyes at each other, and I never saw them hold hands. Maybe when they were young they acted in love. Life was hard in Ireland. Every time Da thought he was getting ahead he got kicked back down."

"There's Zander." Declan increased his speed.

Zander nodded at them both.

"I'm sorry Dawn has taken over the wagon at the moment. I know it's for all five of us." Heath was surprised they hadn't complained to him yet.

Zander shrugged. "After all she's been through, I can't begrudge her. Besides, we never were inside the wagon. Our things are in it and it's our home while we're out here."

"Don't worry about Luella and me. We like the privacy of

the tent. They'll work out the chores or whatever it is women do." Declan smiled.

"Remind Luella she can ride when she wants to. Looks like I'll be driving for a bit. I noticed Dawn shakes when other men are around her. She knows she's safe with you, but she still shakes." Heath said.

"We'd best get back and have something to eat," Zander suggested.

DAWN GRITTED her teeth as they hit another bump. She was foot sore but it might have been easier to walk on her blistered feet than sitting on the bench. "What is that we've been seeing for the last day or so?"

"That's Split Rock," Heath replied.

She studied it for a bit. "You know, it doesn't look like a split at all. I'd say it looks like a giant rock with a piece taken out of the top. Pie-shaped piece."

He laughed. "It does. I hadn't thought of that. Some call it Twin Peaks. It's part of the Rattlesnake Range. From what I hear, we've only got seventy-five miles to go until we hit the South Pass."

"Depending on how the ground is, that could take well over a week," she pointed out, her own experiences traveling west not so far from her mind.

"We're stopping early today to get all the water barrels filled and give the livestock a rest. We're heading into sand again. So you'll want to do your bathing and what not tonight."

"I have clothes to wash. I could wash yours and Zander's for you. I don't have many things."

"It's a tempting offer, but I'd rather you get off your feet and let them heal."

"They've been like this for over nine months. I doubt they'll ever heal."

"I'm going to find other shoes for you, somewhere."

"With so many belongings and furniture on the side of the trail maybe we'll get lucky."

"I'll see if any Indians want to trade tonight."

She widened her eyes. "Indians?"

"Sometimes when we stop, bands come and trade. I figure they'd be around before the Sweetwater runs through a canyon. Heard there wasn't much room. And we'll need to drive our wagons single file through there. If a wagon breaks we won't be able to get around it."

"You certainly know a lot."

"I listen and ask questions and I've read the Pioneer Guide book many times over."

She looked to her left and saw tee pees. It looked like a whole village full of Indians were camped not too far away. Dawn put her hand around his arm and held on tight. "Indians."

"They are supposed to be friendly." He put his hand on top of hers for a brief moment.

The wagons ahead of them began to slow. Her heart beat painfully fast. Blood rushed through her ears, blocking out all other sound. She quickly climbed over the seat into the back of the wagon.

They can't see me. But what if they know to look for me?

Kills Many wasn't the type to let anyone get away from him. Did he still think her dead? There were many different bands of Indians but she wasn't sure who was friendly with the Lakota.

Her body shook and dread filled her as the wagon came to a stop. Now what was she supposed to do?

She waited while Heath unhitched the oxen. She had her knife in her hand while she listened. It was hard to hear if anything was unusual with all the noise the settlers made.

"Dawn, are you in there?" Cora yelled at the wagon.

Dawn crawled to the back. "I don't like the look of those Indians. I'm not coming out of the wagon until we are far from here."

"Would you mind watching Essie? Luella and I are going to see what they have to trade."

"It's not a good idea."

Cora handed Essie to her. "I understand why you feel this way. But the Captain says he knows them. You will be here when I come back for my baby, won't you?"

"Of course." As she smiled down at the baby girl, Dawn hardly noticed Cora leaving. Essie was so beautiful. She ran her hand over her soft hair and then a finger over her eyebrows. She touched the tiny lips and admired the little hand. It made her happy and sad at the same time. Her heart felt like it was in a vise, but she couldn't stop gazing at Essie. Patricia would have been older, but she'd died when she was about the same age as Essie was now.

She held her in her arms and sang while rocking back and forth. She heard a noise right next to the wagon and moved away from the back. She scooted until she was in the very middle of the wagon. Her knife lay next to her. She listened again but whoever it was must have walked away.

Dawn had often wondered if Patricia had lived how would she have fared living with the Lakota? The only conclusion she had ever reached was that Patricia would have suffered a great deal. There was a chance they would have adopted her or a greater chance they would have killed her for crying on the trek to their camp. At least this way, Dawn knew where her body was.

She would welcome another baby. She just didn't trust any man to allow him close enough. Warmth filled her body.

Well…except for one, but he wasn't looking for a wife. He was a good friend, and she didn't want it going any further. What if she couldn't stand for him to touch her? It wasn't worth taking the chance.

She stopped her musing. The noise came again. Then she saw buckskin clad legs climb into the wagon. She grabbed her knife. There was no way she was going back. She put Essie on the blanket behind her.

"It's me, Swift Eagle." He grabbed her arm as she tried to stab him in the heart. Then he took the knife away.

Dawn slumped. "I thought— Does Kills Many still think I'm dead?"

"He believes you have strong magic and is glad you left. He thinks you came back to life to get revenge on him." He smiled at her. "That must be Cora's child."

"Yes. Her name is Essie."

"I know what Kills Many did to your girl. I am sorry." He reached out and touched her shoulder. "Are you doing fine here with your people?"

"Yes, Luella and Cora have been very kind."

He hesitated for a moment. "How is Luella?"

Dawn smiled. "You probably know better than me if you followed us this far."

"Your hair is very pretty without the buffalo grease and charcoal."

"Thank you."

"Tell your man—"

"I don't have a man."

"Yes, you just don't know it yet. Tell the one who sleeps under your wagon that trading with the Cheyenne is fine but to watch the cattle and horses. That is why they are really here."

"What about people?" Her lips quivered.

"You stay hidden. Word of the woman with powerful

magic is a story being told. I also wanted to give these to you." He reached inside his shirt and drew out the pair of baby booties Patricia had been wearing. Dawn had knitted them and laughed at how small they were. Lincoln thought a baby couldn't be that small."

Her eyes shimmered when he handed them to her. "Thank you."

He nodded. "I'm going to visit with Luella and I need to get back to the tribe for good this time. You have a future in front of you. A good future."

Dawn nodded.

"Don't forget to stay hidden." He turned and jumped out of the wagon.

She didn't hear any commotion so he probably hadn't been seen. He was a handsome man with a kind heart. She hoped that he had a good future too.

Luella and Cora came back with beads and a few silver bracelets. Cora took Essie and shared her joyous news of another child growing inside of her. Dawn smiled and hugged Cora like any normal woman would do.

"Swift Eagle is looking for you, Luella. He said for me to stay hidden and the Cheyenne are going to steal the horses and cattle." She watched as Cora and Luella exchanged worried looks.

"Are you fine here by yourself?" Luella asked. "I need to find Swift Eagle."

"Of course, and you won't have to look hard. He'll find you."

The women left and tears trailed down Dawn's face. Cora was so very blessed, and it was right to be happy for her, but in Dawn's heart she felt like dying. She looked at the yellow baby booties, held them to her chest and rocked back and forth, quietly weeping.

She felt the wagon sway as someone sat on the bench behind her. She didn't turn. She didn't care.

"I'm to make sure you stay hidden." She knew the voice and just nodded, relaxing some.

"Are you all right?" Heath asked.

She didn't answer, and he climbed into the wagon. There wasn't much room but he managed to sit down and turn her. "What is it?" He put his arms around her and pulled her onto his lap. "Sweetness, what is it?"

"Cora is going to have another child. And I am happy for her, but...sad for me. Swift Eagle brought these to me." She showed him the knitted baby socks. "I made these for my baby." She couldn't talk anymore. She wept loudly. It seemed so strange to be able to cry so. No Cheyenne would think she was in the wagon with all the noise she was making.

He stroked her back, and she cried for a long time. She would never be free of the Indians or what they had done. She wasn't fit to live among others. She should seek out a white trapper. She'd seen plenty of them, and some weren't so bad.

"I'm sorry you're the one who is always stuck with me. It'll only be until we get to the fort. Perhaps I could get a job there?"

"No."

"No?"

"The only jobs are usually for women who will share themselves for money at night while they do laundry during the day. You have so many other choices."

She nodded. "I could marry one of the half-breed guides I've heard about or one of the trappers. I've heard them offer to trade for me so they won't be lonely all winter."

"Look at me."

She raised her head and met his clear water-blue eyes.

46

She'd seen few men with red hair in her life. He sure was a handsome one.

"Dawn, you've been married surely you know those trappers don't want a woman to have a conversation with. You deserve better."

"I had better. I had my turn at happiness, and my turn is over. Life is funny that way and we never know what will happen next. I don't think you get more than one time at happiness. I'm just not sure how far away from others I will have to live. I'm not acceptable, and I understand. It wasn't anything I did, but I can't change it. Perhaps I can get a piece of land and make my own way. I know I can survive."

"We'll figure something out. Right now we have to be alert and keep you safe. I can't imagine how you survived. I see the marks on your arms. Which reminds me, let me see your feet."

"I don't think it proper."

"Just show me."

She hesitated and then showed him the bottoms of her feet. She knew he'd be shocked but though they always hurt, there wasn't a thing she could do about it. They were full of cuts, blisters, open wounds, scars. Even her toes were starting to curl up from the small shoes she'd been given.

"How in the world do you walk? It pains me to look at them. You stay put I'll be right back."

She nodded. She wasn't supposed to leave the wagon. She took her Bible out and read. Sometimes she had no idea what things meant but reading them soothed her battered soul. She still held on to the booties as she took a deep breath. Then another. It was sweet of Swift Eagle to bring them to her. How had he known she needed to have them? Looking at them was hard. They represented the worst day of her life, but they were also the only physical reminder she had of her precious child. Lincoln used to tell her Patricia was perfect.

She had been a sweet child, Lincoln a good man. He'd provided for them and he'd always put her happiness above his. He had died so, so young.

The wagon rocked and Heath was back. He had whiskey and bandages with him. Dawn's breath caught. It was going to be painful.

"I get to drink the whiskey right?"

He smiled. "Just how many times have you had whiskey?"

"I never counted."

He opened the jug. "Here, smell it before you take a swig."

She took the jug, sniffed it, and shuddered. "Why do men like to drink it?"

"I actually like it. But I grew up on the stuff. That is, until the Great Hunger. Now give me a foot."

"It won't matter, they won't heal. I had to stand in a bed of coals once. The skin has never healed after that. But every rock I step on hurts twice as much as before. I appreciate your efforts. Oohh, that hurts!" As he poured the alcohol over her foot, the pain was so intense her eyes watered and she couldn't breathe. "Wash it off! Please!"

He just grabbed her other foot and did the same.

"Heath Leary, you are the very devil. Leave me be!" She squirmed and tried to turn this way and that, but he held her ankles. She managed to get one foot free and kicked his face before giving it a thought. She froze in place and grabbed a cloth to wipe away the blood from his nose. "It's not broken."

"It sure feels as though it is. I did a bit of boxing in Ireland to make a bit of money, and I've never been as hurt as this." He grabbed the cloth from her and held it to his nose.

If she could have gone somewhere out of his sight she would have. She'd thought for a moment he'd hit her back, but he didn't. He waited for the bleeding to stop and put down the cloth.

He then soaked a clean cloth in some water before he

washed her feet. He was so gentle and it made her feel even worse.

"I didn't mean to. I'm so sorry. It does prove that I shouldn't be around people. I'm dangerous. Please forgive me."

"It was my own fault for trying to restrain you. You have one powerful kick." He gave her a lopsided smile. "Now I'm going to scrub your feet with lye soap, and it won't feel the best, but the worst is over."

She nodded. When he said scrub he'd meant scrub. He lathered the strong soap on a brush and scrubbed. It hurt, but he could have scrubbed much harder. She wondered how he restrained himself. He was the type that was quick to anger, but he didn't react. It took a lot to hold back and there was much respect for a man who could do it.

Finally he rolled bandages around her feet. "You look worried, sweetness."

She laughed and put her hand over her mouth to stop. "How can you call me sweetness after that?"

He chuckled and winced. Then he turned serious. "Because that's what you are to me, sweetness and light. You gone through and seen the worst one person can do to another, yet you have a sweet giving spirit that draws me like a light on a stormy sea. You are very different from anyone I've ever known. I can see your strength, yet there is a bit of vulnerability to you. You remind me of all the sorrow, suffering, and shame my people live through, yet they are willing to fight another day. You are like a beautiful warrior ready to defend her people and country. But I'm just going on and on."

She stared into his eyes, and for a moment she felt like the person he described. Her face heated, and she clasped and unclasped her hands.

"Oh I forgot I bought you something." He reached out to

the wagon bench and brought in a pair of moccasins. "This has nothing to do with Indians, all right? They are just supposed to be comfortable, and Swift Eagle suggested I get them for you."

She took them and examined them, from the stitching to the pretty beading. "It's one of the nicest gifts I've ever received. Perhaps my feet will heal after all. You are a kind man Heath Leary. Thank you."

"You're not going to cry again, are you?"

She shook her head as she wiped a few tears away.

"Good. Tonight we'll both have rifles just in case they've somehow found you. I'll cover the back while you cover the front. Do you still have your knife?"

She nodded and a shudder went through her. "We leave in the morning?"

"As early as possible. Extra food is being prepared today because we are not stopping tomorrow. Then our next hurdle is the three crossings."

"What is that?"

"There are two ways we can go according to Captain London. We can go through days of sand or we can cross the river three times in one big crossing and avoid the dry sand. There are two islands so crossing from the bank to island one is one crossing and crossing from the island to the other island is two crossings and crossing from there to the opposite bank makes it three crossings. The islands are tiny so you hardly get going before you go to the next one. It's supposed to save the oxen a lot of hard pulling. Some say it's dangerous, but many have made it across."

"The crossing sounds like the way we should go."

"Do you swim, lass?"

"I sure do. Lincoln and I..." She picked up the booties again. "I'm a good swimmer."

CHAPTER FIVE

*S*till about three hours remained until sunset, and Heath could feel trepidation throughout the camp. He'd left the wagon to stretch his legs and see if any of the plans had changed. He saw several people peeking out from their wagons. He bet the Cheyenne could see them too as their camp wasn't very far away.

Harrison, Declan, Zander, and numerous other drovers each drove about five head of cattle to the three crossings and swam the animals across. All that was left were the horses and the animals that pulled the wagons. Other men stood holding their rifles where they could be seen by the Cheyenne. The wagons were all packed and little by little the livestock were being moved closer to the circle.

The women had all the children inside the wagons as they put out their cooking fires. As soon as it was dark, the animals would be harnessed and the train would ride out with the men on horseback behind ready to fight if needed.

Swift Eagle had said it was unlikely they'd be pursued since there would be many more trains passing by.

"Same rascals were right past Independence Rock last

year. We lost three head of cattle, and one man was injured. That Indian friend has sure been a big help to us." Captain London drew on his pipe. "He sure has. My last pass through this area the Indians here were just trading. I had no problems with them. Of course they might not be the same ones."

Finally it was dark, and Heath helped Cora with her oxen. Luella would ride with her ready to shoot her rifle. Then Heath yoked the oxen for the wagon Dawn was in. She lay low in the wagon with a rifle. Heath had his close at hand in the front.

Slowly they left the circle, one by one. Heath heard a commotion behind him. "Can you see what's going on?"

"Three armed Cheyenne are speaking to Harrison and two other men. One, I think, is a scout. There's a lot of pointing and talking." She was quiet for a few minutes. "The Cheyenne rode back to their village. The fear of sickness seemed to have worked."

"Whole families have been wiped out by the sickness we bring with us."

"Yes, I've seen it and was punished for it."

Heath almost jumped. She was sitting right behind him now and he'd never heard her move. "I think we should ask God for his continued protection."

"Yes, I've been reading and praying a lot today. When it seems like no one else understands, God does."

Heath nodded. "God is easy to talk to."

They traveled in silence for the rest of the way. Heath had one ear cocked, listening for horses' hooves or a gunshot. They had to go single file due to the narrowing of canyon. It was easy to imagine the Cheyenne standing at the top of the ridge ready to pick them off. Fortunately, all was well.

They arrived at the place where they would cross the Sweetwater River. They'd start crossing at first light. It was a long eerie night. It was almost as though he could hear Dawn holding her breath.

When the sun rose, Heath heard speculation about Dawn's part in the whole thing. There was talk of tying her up again. When would people stop? He shook his head and rolled out from under the wagon. If he'd heard it, then so had Dawn. He glared at all who glanced his way. Why couldn't they just stay with their wagons?

The signal to go was given and many had to hurry to their wagons. Didn't they even see the danger? Dawn sat in the wagon with the rifle in her lap as she put together a few biscuits and bacon together for Heath to eat while they continued through. Somehow, she had cold coffee for him too. He smiled his thanks and jumped up into the front of the wagon ready to go.

The first wagon started across the three crossings. The water was strong and the oxen visibly fought to stay upright. It was slow going, and some drivers were impatient. One wagon driver yelled and whipped the oxen, and the next thing they knew the wagon tipped on its side and then it was gone, taken away by the river, oxen and all.

From behind him, Dawn gasped. "Was there anyone inside that wagon?"

"I'm not entirely sure. Between the livestock and guard duty, I haven't had much time to socialize. I think he had a wife and a couple young ones. I just don't understand." Heath shook his head sadly. "You'd think people would listen to the captain."

They heard crying, and many in the wagon party sounded fearful.

"Life is so unpredictable," she said. "Out in the West, one wrong move can get you killed. I loved living in our settlement. There weren't very many people and I liked it that way. It was my downfall, though. There weren't enough people to help protect others."

"Sometimes no matter what you do you can't stop things from happening." Heath thought of his heartbreak of having to leave his family behind. He knew he'd never see them again and he prayed that they didn't suffer more than they already had. Neither he nor Declan had heard much about what was going on in Ireland. He just hoped that this year's potato crop was successful. It had been two years in a row of the blight. How many had died? If he judged just by his county, it was at least a third.

"Ready?"

He turned his head for a moment and smiled at her. "Don't you worry; I won't ask you to show me how well you swim. If there is a problem, get as far away from the wagon as you can and use your knife to cut off your skirt. It will become too heavy with water and drown you."

"We'll be just fine." Her smile of confidence made his heart swell. "Here we go."

He concentrated on getting the oxen to the opposite bank, but he could picture her huddled behind him. Up the bank they went and across the island, down one bank and up another until they were almost there. The last bank was almost too muddy to get any traction, but they made it. He kept driving until he reached his brother and Zander, who were still waiting for Harrison to drive Luella and Cora over.

They were quickly joined by the other wagon and one of the scouts had Zander and Declan ride ahead making sure the livestock was still moving. There would be no resting. But that was fine as long as his family and friends were all right.

"How long do you think I need to stay in here?" Dawn asked.

"Until the captain says otherwise. You're not missing

much. The ground is soggy, but it's better than deep sand. It looks like there will be plenty for the oxen to eat when we stop."

"Why didn't we stop when that wagon turned over? We all could have said a few words or perhaps someone should have ridden down along the bank to look for survivors."

"From what I was told, no one survives that crossing if their wagon smashes to pieces. I guess the captain wanted everyone to keep going so we are farther away from the Cheyenne. I wish I had more answers for you."

He watched a few of the women walking and the boggy ground sucked their shoes like mud. It made for hard going.

"What do you think will happen to me?"

"What do you mean?" he asked with a growing sense of unease.

"I'm getting stronger, and I know people have been talking about me. I figure the captain has plans to drop me off somewhere. When do we get to the next fort?"

Drop her off? Leave her somewhere? He'd heard nothing of the sort. He shook his head. "I don't know. Is that what you want to do? I thought you changed your mind about trying to find a job at a fort."

"It's not as though I have many choices." Dawn spread her hands in a rare show of helplessness. "Besides, Luella should be the one in this wagon with Declan driving. I have looked over the single men and none appeal to me. I may have to change my mind and take the first offer I get. Do you even think there will *be* offers?"

There would be offers, all right, but not the type she'd appreciate. He'd talk to the captain and see what he thought.

"It would have to be someone that can find me a place to sleep. I could walk most of the way."

"I think for now staying with us will be best. We make you feel safe, don't we? If you end up sleeping under a wagon

I doubt you'll sleep at all. It's fine as things are, plus Declan and Luella seem to like their tent. Let's just get your feet healed, and then we can talk to the captain and see what he suggests." He wished he could have seen her expression. But he needed all of his concentration driving through the bog. It seemed like hours before they were told to stop.

———

DAWN NEEDED SOMETHING TO DO. If she could find some material she could make some clothes. She waited at the end of the wagon for the captain to decide if she could come out or not. Sometimes she was so restless and to imagine just a bit ago she wished for time to rest. Her feet were bad, but the rest of her was healing. Her back didn't hurt as bad as it had, and she hadn't been burned with a lit stick either.

There was so much more to what had happened to her, but she'd never be able to speak of it. It haunted her though. She blamed herself so many times but really she had no power. She'd always want to know that she was allowed to have an opinion. Her mother had taught many of the children at the settlement. It wasn't a formal education but she could read the classics as well as any. Her mind was quicker at figures than Lincoln's had been. He'd finally learned to just tell her the numbers and she'd give him an answer.

She wasn't what she's call a beauty. Lincoln had thought so but she looked into the mirror and saw many of her flaws. Did all people do that? Now she didn't want to know what she looked like. Hopefully bad enough no man would want to touch her.

She waited and waited and finally Harrison stopped to speak with her.

"The captain thinks it's fine if you want to get out of the

wagon. We are to all stay alert though." He chuckled "Don't worry, we'll keep an eye on you."

She smiled, and when he lifted his hands up she slowly stood, flinching as he lifted her to the ground. He then grabbed two crates and set them down. "One for you and one for your feet. I can only imagine how they must hurt."

"I'll be fine. Do you know where I might be able to get some fabric and sewing items? I can work to pay back the cost. It's just so boring sitting all the time, and I'm good at sewing. I need some clothes." Her face heated. Was she being too bold in asking?

"I'll get my wife on it. She sews too. She'll be heading over after she feeds Essie."

"Thank you, Harrison. I appreciate your kindness."

"I'll see you later."

She watched him walk toward his wagon. Everyone was gathering around a few of the men. They were all laughing, and they seemed excited.

"Wonder what that's all about?" Heath said as he slipped something cold down the back of her dress.

She squirmed. "What is that?"

"It's ice." He showed her a bucket and it had ice in it.

"I was thinking it was a bit on the warm side."

"I don't know the why or how of it but if you dig down a bit you find ice. One of the drovers told me this is the only place he's ever seen it." He grabbed two tin cups and filled them with water from the water barrel. The he put a bit of ice in each.

She took a sip as soon as he handed it to her. "Why does water taste better when it's ice cold?"

Luella and Cora hurried to their side. "Is it the ice?" Luella asked.

Dawn nodded. "Try some in the water."

They couldn't stop exclaiming about it and wondering

why ice would be underground like that. Dawn watched all of their happy animated faces. This was how life was supposed to be. The contrast was overwhelming.

Cora handed Essie to Harrison and went to their wagon. When she came back she had yard goods, needles and thread, and she even had buttons. "If you need any help let me know."

Dawn's eyes started to puddle. "You've all been more than kind to me."

Heath shifted until he was almost next to her. She tried not to tense up, but she couldn't help it. She really appreciated his thoughtfulness. He was always there for her. "I could put that in the wagon."

"Could you grab a quilt and a pair of scissors for me? I'm going to sit on the ground and cut the pieces so I can start."

He nodded and got what she needed. He laid out the quilt and then swept her up into his arms. Carefully he placed her on the quilt."

"You know that everyone is staring, don't you? Including all the single girls."

He turned red and glanced up. "They really are nosey. I guess your life is more exciting than theirs. How could it be any other way with me around?"

"Go drink your ice water."

He smiled and stood back up. "If you insist."

He was good for her soul but she practically cringed the whole time he carried her. Would she ever be normal? She took the scissors and cut out her pieces. She would do herself some good if she didn't think about him. It would only lead to trouble and heartache. She wasn't up to dealing with either.

Supper wouldn't be ready for about another hour. Dawn was quick to cut out her pieces. She was visualizing the dress in her head.

Cora stood at the edge of the quilt. "Would you mind if I lay Essie down on the quilt? She'll probably sleep the whole time. Harrison and I haven't had any time alone to talk."

Dawn's heart ached as Cora put the baby down close to her.

"Thank you!" she whispered. Cora then grabbed Harrison's hand and they walked away together.

Zander sat down on one of the crates. He was sitting so he was facing her. "I don't think it's talking they have on their mind."

She didn't look up and didn't respond.

"Well, what do you think they are up too?" he asked her.

The blood drained from her face. She already knew why married people would want to have a bit of privacy but it wasn't something openly talked about. She just shook her head quickly and threaded a needle.

"You are wound up tight. I see how you never relax. I think behind your smiles you are afraid. What did they do to you?" he pressed. "I just want to know."

Taking a deep breath, she closed her eyes. When she opened them, Zander was still staring, expecting her to answer. Her heart raced. He made her feel trapped. As quickly as she could, she stood and ran the few steps to the wagon and practically vaulted inside it. With shaking hands, she cinched the canvas up in the back and then shifted and did the front.

Her body shook, and suddenly she felt cold. It had been a mistake to leave the wagon. No one wanted to know her; they just wanted to know how she was tortured.

Dread flooded her body, leaving ice in her veins. *Oh my!* She had left Essie alone on the quilt. She was a horrible person.

As silently as possible, she went to the back of the wagon and peeked out. Zander now sat on the quilt with the baby.

She looked fine. Dawn's hands trembled as she considered whether she should go to the baby. Why had she left her?

It would never work. Just being around other people exhausted her. The whole time she was with the Lakota she had wanted to be free. But she'd never be free of the questions, the sly looks, the gossip, and the hatred

There was no grand party for her return. No one was happy to see her. She wasn't even going to a place she was familiar with. Maybe she could get back to the settlement and see if anyone had survived.

Not many who were spared death on the first day had made it to the Indian camp. There had been three women, one man, and four children from a settlement not too far from theirs. She wasn't sure of their ages but she thought them to be a boy of six years old and another boy who was perhaps ten. The two girls were sisters who appeared to be about twelve and maybe fifteen.

The children belonged to the three other women. The man didn't belong to anyone. She'd been pushed to the ground when she first was brought to the group. The wait wasn't very long. They tied their hands and added what amounted to a lead line to each of the prisoners. They had to keep up with the horses or be dragged.

At first they traveled at a regular walking speed then they began to go faster and faster until she was out of breath trying to keep up and on her feet. She'd stumbled many times but didn't fall. Others weren't as lucky. They finally stopped on a high hill. One of the Indians made a motion for them to all sit under a tree. Dawn had barely caught her breath when the youngest boy, who had been crying loudly, and his mother, who was growing hysterical, were yanked up.

Kills Many slit the boy's throat with his large knife and they dragged the mother off. There were a few screams and then silence. She'd never forget that strange silence. She didn't want to hear more screams, but silence was so much worse.

Then it was time to go again, but she saw them take the little boy's scalp. She was almost sick but she willed herself to be strong and quiet. There was no food and little rest the next two days. One of the Indians grabbed up the younger girl and rode away. Dawn never saw the girl or the Indian again.

The girl's sister, Jenny was beside herself but Dawn did what she could to keep her from crying. They were already annoyed with the girl's mother, Peg. She was a nice woman but her grief got the better of her. When next they stopped, they had treated Peg brutally. It was like sport to them. Peg's cries only made them more brutal as they laughed loudly. Through it all, Dawn held Jenny in her arms telling her not to make a sound.

Dawn shivered. She didn't want to remember any more of that awful day.

"Dawn? Are you all right?" Luella called.

"I just need to be in the wagon. I thought I was ready, but I'm not. I'm sorry. Is Essie still sleeping?"

"Yes she is. I'll have Heath bring you dinner and your sewing when he gets back. The world can be a very scary place."

A tear rolled down Dawn's face. "Yes it can. Thank you for understanding."

Dawn rolled herself into a ball and cried. After she was done, she found her Bible and spent the next hour or so reading. It always soothed her, but it didn't take her horrendous memories away. They would always be with her. She wasn't fit to be a friend or a wife. She couldn't be counted on. How could she have left Essie?

Lord, I don't know how to help myself. I'm grateful I'm free and the people I'm with do care about me but I don't feel free. What I

lost can never be gotten back. What's done is done, and I under-
stand that. Don't allow me to put others in danger. Something
could have happened to Essie. A snake could have... Please help me
to move forward instead of looking back. It's so hard. The memories
come back on their own. I love you.

The front of the wagon was being opened, and she knew it must be Heath. He popped his head in. "I heard Zander put his foot in his mouth again." He opened the canvas a bit more and handed her the sewing. "I'll have supper for you soon."

She nodded. There was no use trying to look cheerful. He'd know it to be a lie.

"Sit tight."

She sewed as she waited and then took the food when he handed it to her.

"Try to eat a little at least. I have early guard duty. Don't scratch the floor until the second half of the night." He gave her a cheerful smile. "I know this must be hard for you. The only thing I know is each day you try to survive and it'll get easier. I'll be back later."

Surviving, he was right about, but he wasn't right about it getting any easier.

CHAPTER SIX

*H*eath was livid. He paced back and forth until his guard duty was over. He had a few words for Zander. Usually he was a great friend, but he had been beyond disrespectful to Dawn.

He watched as other guards were relieved and it made him angry. Finally, Zander came along with his rifle. He was rubbing his eyes and stumbled on the uneven ground.

"All quiet?" he asked as he approached.

"Unless I release some of my anger on you it is," snarled Heath.

"What's wrong?" Zander seemed truly perplexed but then a grin slid over his face. "Oh, I bet that Indian lover has you wanting to do her bidding. I think I need to rescue you before you do something that ties you to that woman for life." He frowned.

"If you had taken the time to get to know her instead of questioning her as though she were a criminal, you might like her. She lost her husband and baby in the attack. It's not like she ran away to an Indian village and asked to live there." Anger seethed just below the surface. "She was a captive. I know you've heard the rumors of what goes on with captives. Why would you think she'd want to tell you? It's hurtful to her."

Zander retreated a step and held out his hands in surrender. "I'll apologize tomorrow. I had no idea our plans for the future would get to be so complicated. Declan has Luella, and now you seem taken with Dawn. See you in the morning."

Heath walked away. Maybe Zander thought that since he wasn't their brother, they'd change their minds about the ranch. He didn't seem to realize how loyal they were to each other. Heath shuddered. Had he been as grating to Declan and Luella? His gut told him perhaps an apology was owed to them.

The camp was quiet except for the lowing of the cattle and oxen. They would probably make as much distance tomorrow as possible. That wasn't good for Dawn's feet. Maybe they could pad the bottom of the moccasins. It might not work, but he needed to try. She might say she wanted to stay in the wagon, but she'd probably want to walk at least a bit tomorrow.

Eventually, she'd forget about what happened. He should have thought to get her things she needed. She'd gotten some castoffs from a few of the women. He should have tried to trade for a dress in addition to the moccasins.

He grabbed his bedroll that he'd placed next to the wagon wheel and rolled it out under the wagon. Then he followed. The first thing he heard was her fingernail scratching at the floorboards. He smiled and felt strangely warm inside. He needed his sleep. She should have slept hours ago. But maybe she couldn't sleep. Thoughts haunted a person at times.

SHE COULD BE BRAVE, very brave. She'd stood her ground against the Lakota a few times. She could go and help with breakfast. Her feet were still feeling raw, but she'd be able to contribute in some way.

She dressed and braided her hair. Then she put on her moccasins. She'd change the bandages while she was riding in the wagon. She looked out finding no one around but the fire was going. She carefully climbed down. The ground was a bit spongy.

Putting down the tailgate she put everything needed into the coffee pot and set it on a metal grate she'd laid over hot coals. The bread dough had been made after supper and put into the wagon. Most likely by Luella.

Dawn put the dough in a Dutch oven and placed it among the coals. Then she mixed the ingredients for fried corn cakes. They were out of bacon, so she pulled some of the dried beef out. She gathered some fresh sage and mixed it into the corn cake batter. Maybe someone would be lucky at hunting today. Looking west she didn't see much of anything. Certainly not good lands for a successful hunting party. The prospect of fresh meat dimmed.

Luella walked out of the tent, stretching and yawning. "Oh! Hello," she greeted. "I didn't think anyone was out here. Declan went to check the feet of one of the Oxen he has a concern about, and he made the fire. Looks like you've been busy."

"I need to move around to regain all of my strength and I'm tired of the wagon." Dawn remembered to smile. "This I could do without having to walk too much."

Luella took out a few crates for sitting. "Heath didn't paint a pretty picture when he told us about them. To have been in such pain for that length of time… You are a brave woman. I would have refused to walk."

"People always think of what they would do, but when

faced with walking or death, walking was preferable. They did prize bravery. It was not tolerated for a man to be weak. A brave woman was respected. Sometimes I wonder if I was brave or just stupid. But I'm still alive. Few who were captured with me even made it."

"I'm glad you made it. What is that you put in the batter?"

Dawn smiled. Luella seemed to accept her. "Sage, it will give the corn cakes a good taste. I thought something a bit different would be nice since we're out of bacon."

"We'll be at Fort Hall in a few days. We did bring the dried meat to eat." Luella took over and fried up the corn cakes, insisting, "You need to sit for a bit."

The others in their party all showed up, and each expressed happiness to see Dawn. She turned and Zander was behind her. Her breath caught as she eyed him warily. She still had her knife on her.

"I'm sorry as can be about yesterday," he said softly. "I'm not very sensitive to others' feelings at times. I don't know why, but it happens. Forgive me."

"Of course." She turned back to the fire. He was sorry, but he had an excuse. Not the most trustworthy of qualities. Excuses were crutches that weren't needed.

"We need to watch how much water we use. We'll be making a steady climb all day and the livestock will need the water more than you," Captain London said as he helped himself to a cup of coffee. "Don't let looks deceive you. We will be climbing. It doesn't look like much of an incline but the oxen feel it. We'll camp near the Sweetwater tonight, and we have a few more crossings to make. Also make sure your oxen are grazing. They won't eat during the day but if we see grass, we stop and encourage them to graze for a bit. Stay with them at night and be sure… ahh, you already know all this. Can I get something to eat?"

Heath's lips twitched, and he gazed right at her. Keeping from smiling was hard, but she did it.

Later, after everything was packed up, she swatted his shoulder." What, are you a school boy trying to make me laugh?"

"I had fun, so maybe it was like being a school boy." They both laughed. He looked into her eyes and quickly looked away. They would never be more than just friends.

She sat in front of the fire sewing while Heath checked all the leather needed to hitch up the animals and drive them. It was a nice silence, a comfortable one. But then she glanced up and saw someone dart back behind a wagon. She furrowed her brow.

"What is it? What's wrong?" asked Heath.

"I saw someone. He darted behind a wagon when I looked that way. I've seen it before, but with so many people it's hard to tell if they are just walking by. Am I really so fascinating? Or am I more of a side show to them?" She shook her head. "I have noticed that I seem to panic easily. I probably overreacted to Zander. I don't know how to act in polite society anymore."

"From what I heard you didn't overreact. He has a need for a home. A permanent home. And with each addition to our little group, he feels threatened. He thinks his dreams will fail. He spent a long time in an orphanage and from what I gather it wasn't a pleasant experience."

He stared up at the sky for a moment. "I think you are going just fine. I was worried when you were curled up in the wagon but you came around. We'd best get ready to leave. We don't want to be out of captain London's good graces."

She nodded and gathered the crates and her sewing. They were all put into the back of the wagon. She used a shovel and tossed dirt on the fire. Lastly, she climbed into the back.

When Heath climbed up and sat on the bench she relaxed. It was always better when he drove. They'd have to drive the wagon anyway, but somehow she felt like an inconvenience when she was in it. She would walk today and she would get stronger.

It was still early in the day when the bog dried out, and all that could be seen was sand. Heath stopped the wagon and let Dawn off.

"I'll keep an eye out," he told her. "If you need me just signal."

She gave him a smile. He was protective of her, and she liked it.

She started walking. The sky was cloudless and the sun was scorching. The air was hot and dry. Now she knew why Heath and Declan filled a barrel full of buffalo chips. They'd need them for fires. If they made good time they'd come to the Sweetwater River again. It was hard going in the sand, but there were no hard rocks to step on.

"Dawn, wait up!"

She turned, and Luella was waving at her and beside her, Cora smiled. Dawn waited to see what they wanted. Then it occurred to her they wanted to walk with her. Her heart warmed and her eyes were misty.

"This sand is getting into my eyes too," Cora said.

"We're keeping our eyes open for another wagon," Luella informed her.

"I don't need to be in the wagon anymore. I know that the wagon is yours. It's not right for me to ride and sleep in the wagon when you should be."

"Dawn, you haven't inconvenienced me at all. I told you about looking for a wagon so you would know that we are your family now and there is a place for you."

Dawn stared at the grains of sand blowing across the terrain. Part of their family? Could that be true? "Thank you.

It's been a while since I've had good people in my life. Swift Eagle chose well."

"Oh look, two wagons have pulled off," Cora said.

All the other wagons had come to an almost stop as they drove around the stopped wagons. "Will anyone help them?" Dawn asked.

"It depends. People are expected to be able to fix their own wagons. It could be sickness. We'll pass too close if it's sickness." Cora held Essie closer.

"We'll have to go around from the other side. We'll be a bit farther from the wagons though," Dawn suggested.

They walked perpendicular from the road and went around the wagons.

"Look Cora, it's Eddie. He has a broken wheel. That's fixed easy enough," Luella commented.

Cora laughed. "He didn't bring any spare parts and didn't think that keeping your wagon and livestock in good condition pertained to him. Who else stopped?"

Movement on the ground caught Dawn's attention, and she threw her knife so fast it made Cora scream.

"Oh you saved my life," whispered Cora, staring at the sand. "I thought snakes went away when people were around."

Dawn bent and retrieved her knife. "I'm not sure that's true. I've seen more than my share."

Cora handed Essie to Luella. Tears rolled down her face. "I could have left Essie motherless." Her body began to shake. Dawn pulled her close in a big hug.

Fortunately, Harrison was driving in the back of the line and pulled off. He jumped down and ran to them. "Cora?" She looked up at him and exchanged Dawn's hug for his.

"We'll keep walking," Luella said as she took Dawn's hand in hers. The two walked on with Essie in Luella's arms.

"I figured they needed a bit of privacy. Facing death can be hard to take."

"It is," Dawn answered tonelessly, only with great determination pushing back the memories of her time as a captive.

"I'm sorry. Of course you know. I'm going to treat you as I would any family member, and I'll end up saying the wrong things at times but tip-toing around things will make it hard to become close. I won't ask you what happened but I'm here if you need someone to talk to."

"Now I'm going to cry," Dawn whispered. Then Essie began to cry loudly. Luella tried everything to calm the baby. "Here let me try." She took the precious girl into her arms and sighed contently. Essie stared at her with her big eyes and then began to coo at her. Then she yawned and lay her head down on Dawn's shoulder.

Mixed blessings. Dawn missed her own child but holding Essie no longer made her heart hurt; if anything it helped.

Luella peered at the two stopped wagons. "It's that Chuck Klass man who stopped with Eddie." Well they are well matched in temperament. Both are mean. It's best we walked past them the way we did even with the snake."

"Chuck Klass, is the man I see watching me from time to time as well as Eddie. I figured Eddie was just trying to find out more about Cora." Dawn kissed the top of the baby's head. "Essie is such a sweet baby."

"Declan and I haven't announced it yet, but I'm pretty sure I'm with child." Luella blushed.

"That's the best news I've heard in a while. Imagine Declan holding a tiny baby." Dawn smiled.

"Declan is a big, tall man," said Luella. "It will be nice to see. We're not making a formal announcement. Too many women have lost their babies on this trip. All the exertion is hard on the body. We got married only a little while before you appeared. So it hasn't been very long. Please don't tell Heath."

"I won't breathe a word. Look, that's Heath. He must have known something was wrong." They walked a bit faster until they got to the stopped wagon.

"What happened? Where is Cora?"

Luella told Heath about the snake.

Heath gazed at Dawn in surprise. "I knew you carried a knife, but…"

"I do know how to use it."

"Where's the snake? You didn't leave it there, did you?"

Dawn scrunched her nose. "I will never eat snake again, and I didn't want the rattle tail either. If I wasn't holding this dear one, I'd have to punch you in the arm."

Heath glanced at Luella and they both laughed softly.

"Did you stop to give us a ride?" Dawn asked.

"Yes I did."

"Dawn, why don't you and Essie get in? I won't add extra weight. I've found that I can walk farther and farther each day."

"But—"

"Dawn you've walked for hours and I know your feet are still healing," Luella strode on.

Heath helped Dawn up.

HE COULDN'T GET over how natural she looked holding the baby. He thought she might not have wanted to have, see, or hold a baby again. Perhaps she was putting the past behind her, at least a bit.

It was getting dark, and they still hadn't stopped. The Oxen looked tired. More than one wagon pulled over. He had enough to take care of. He wasn't willing to stop and help.

"I can hardly see, and Essie needs to be fed."

"I'll hail one of the scouts when I see one."

It wasn't a scout but Harrison who rode up. "I bet she's hungry."

Heath laughed. "We were just thinking the same thing. I'll pull off."

"Just come to a slow crawl. There isn't anyone behind you for at least half a mile. Eddie has been stepping in front of every wagon demanding a wheel. I'm surprised no one has run him over."

Heath slowed and took Essie from Dawn. Dawn's look of pleasure enthralled him. "Here you go, Daddy."

"Dawn, thanks for saving my wife out there." Before she could answer, Harrison swung his horse around and started back.

"You're lovely."

"What do you mean?"

"You seem like…" He shrugged. "I can't think of a way to say this that won't end up with me pushed off the wagon."

A smile came over her face, and she chuckled.

"You have the look of a contented woman, all sweet and pretty. Not that I don't respect your knife throwing skills."

"As long as you know I can throw it a very far way and not miss, I thank you for the compliment. I feel more like a woman than a slave or a thing to be hurt. I think, little by little, I'm learning to trust people."

He put the reins in one hand and took her small calloused one in the other then entwined their fingers. He had no idea why he was doing it. He wanted to be closer to her, but he didn't want to give her the wrong idea. Maybe he could get her married off. There were plenty of unmarried drovers. Many of them planned to stay in Oregon when they got there. He gave her hand a quick squeeze and let go. He felt better having a good plan.

Finally it was time to stop. A grumpier group he'd never heard. Husbands and wives were griping at each other. Kids got in trouble and were scolded, and the youngest of children cried and carried on. Everyone was tired from walking through the sand without a break.

Then someone called out that the river was there. No wonder the oxen were impatient with him. They could smell the water. "I'll be back."

He led the livestock to the water and watched them drink. Zander had the oxen from Harrison's wagon and he stood next to Heath.

"What a day, or so I heard," Zander said.

"We got slowed down a few times. I bet the cattle and horses had an easier time of it." Heath commented.

"We've been here for a long while. I was about to ride back, but the scouts showed up and told me not to. I thought at least one would be riding up and down the train making sure everything was fine." Zander told him.

Declan joined them. "What's this I hear about Dawn killing a rattler?"

"Did you ask Luella? She was there. All I know is it was set on striking Cora and Dawn threw her knife and killed it."

Declan shook his head. "To hear it, she's a hero to some and a dangerous woman to others. She carries a knife?"

"Yes, she does," confirmed Heath with a sharp nod. "She's still scared out of her mind that she will be taken again or attacked by one of our party. They haven't been welcoming at all. In fact, many have threatened to throw her down and have their way with her. I can't figure what's wrong with people. I bet if the wives of these men knew what they were doing and how they were talking, it would come to a stop. While she was with the Indians, all she thought about was escaping. Now that she's free…well, it's very different than she thought it would be. People seem to hate the fact that she survived." He sighed.

"When are you two getting married?" Declan asked. His lips twitched as though he was trying not to laugh.

"I was thinking on that this very day. I'm going to talk to each moral single man and find someone for her."

Zander and Declan glanced at each other and doubled over in laughter.

"Have you looked in the mirror?" Zander ribbed. Declan and Zander continued to laugh.

Heath took his oxen and led them to a grassy spot and took all the tack off them.

He walked back toward the circle when he saw Eddie and Chuck walking each with a grip on one of Dawn's arms. They were dragging her to the center of the circle. Heath raced toward them and stopped short as Tom Simps stepped in front of him.

"Don't take another step, Leary. She's dangerous, and you know it."

"Where is Captain London?"

Simps laughed. "Not here." He grabbed Heath, and before Heath knew it his hands were tied behind his back.

Heath struggled but he couldn't get loose. He frantically looked around until he saw Dawn. Her face was pale, and he saw why she had not been fighting—she was tied too. The look in her eyes was one of hatred such as he'd never seen before.

"What makes her so dangerous? She hasn't bothered anyone!" He needed to find a way to get help.

Chuck Klass reached under her skirt and produced the knife. He held it up in triumph. "I told you so!" he yelled out to the gathering crowd.

The minister tried to step forward but he was pushed

back, and Simps pulled his gun. "I'll kill anyone who interferes with our safety." The whole crowd recoiled, seeming to take a step back.

"What are you going to do with her?" Heath asked. He caught Dawn's gaze and held it. The fear she was trying to hide was there for him to see.

"I was thinking about using this knife on her. She's the type that would slit a white man's throat while he was sleeping," Eddie said confidently.

"I didn't know she was wandering around at night. Where does she go?" Heath asked his voice laced with sarcasm.

"Shut up!" Tom Simps yelled. He took the knife from Chuck and pulled Dawn into a standing position. He turned her around and slit her dress down the back along with her chemise. "It's time she learns what we will do if we catch her again."

He held up the knife and smiled at the crowd.

"Leave her alone!" Heath cried, his voice coming out shrill with his panic.

Simps gave an evil grin. "I'm just going to slice off a few layers of skin to teach her a lesson. She walks among us as if she was decent enough to be with good people. She needs to be chained up!"

There were many murmurs in the crowd. People didn't seem to want to go along with Simps. But not one spoke up.

Simps tore the dress and chemise from her back, and the crowd gasped.

"There is nothing you can do to me that hasn't been already done. Go ahead take your slices of skin. Will you eat them too?" She spat on the ground.

For a moment, all Heath could do was stare. The scars on her back told her story. It was much worse than he'd imagined. How had she survived? He could see where they hit her with a switch, burned her and cut her. His whole being hurt for her.

"Stop this instant!" ordered a strong woman's voice. Della, the minister's wife, walked toward Dawn and Simps. With a stern eye on Simps, she wrapped Dawn in a shawl and led her away. No one spoke as they watched Della take the injured woman back to the wagon.

"Cut me loose!" Heath demanded.

With a feral growl, Simps used Dawn's knife to cut him loose, and then he handed the knife to Heath. He turned walked to his horse and rode away. Heath wished he had time to clobber each of them but they needed more Godliness and less violence. Instead, he raced for the wagon.

Dawn sat on the tailgate with a blank expression on her face. It was almost as though she wasn't really there. He caught Della's gaze, and she shrugged one shoulder.

"Dawn, me darlin' I'm here. No one will hurt you. Look at me, lass."

She blinked but otherwise she showed no sign she heard.

"Mrs. Paul, could you please tell my brother what happened. I know it's not proper, but I'm going to tuck her in and then hold her. I'll be fully dressed and I won't be under the covers with her."

Della took a minute before she nodded. "Do what you must to bring her back to us."

Heath climbed into the wagon and put the straw tick down on the floor and then covered it with a blanket. Then he put a quilt over that. He took out a fresh nightgown for her. Then he eased her into the wagon before he closed the tailgate and cinched the canvas shut.

He bade her to stand and then turned her away from him. With deft movements, he quickly removed her dress and put on her gown—indulging in no lingering looks. Gently, he helped her down onto the mattress and covered her with the quilt. It was short work removing his boots, and then he lay next to her and slowly pulled her to him until her head was on his shoulder. After only a moment's hesitation, he settled both arms around her.

She still hadn't uttered a word, and he was getting worried.

No one interrupted them, but he could hear their friends outside by the fire. Maybe it would make her feel safe hearing them. But she still hadn't moved. She was like a ragdoll. What was he supposed to do? He had thought she'd snap out of it once they were alone. Hopefully, she wasn't out of her mind. He'd seen it happen to a couple of people when tragedy was too much for them. She seemed to drift to sleep, and he eased her onto her side facing away from him then gathered her to him.

Out of all of them, Harrison was the only one to quietly peek into the wagon. If things weren't so serious, Heath would have laughed at their antics. They were concerned, that much was obvious. But all Heath wanted to know was what happened to Simps, Chuck, and Eddie. Where had Captain London been?

CHAPTER SEVEN

*D*awn woke before the sun as was her habit. She didn't move. She wanted to remember this moment forever. It was a blessing to have Heath's arms around her. She'd suffered so much and there had been no one to comfort her. She'd never experience this simple but very big gesture again. It was strange that it didn't feel at all like Lincoln. She was very aware it was Heath holding her.

Lord, please let his dreams come true. I don't really know if he talks to You often, but I know he was raised to be a church going man. He's done so much for me. He's kind and gentle, and he listens without making judgments. He even called me pretty. I know in the big scheme of things it doesn't matter, but I've felt less than pleasing to look at. You granted my wish to be free, so I'll not be asking for anything for myself. Please bless Cora and Luella and their babes. And Lord if something happened to Captain London, please lead him back to us. My love for You is all encompassing. You've been my only friend for a very long time and I thank You with my whole heart for being there for me.

She shifted, and his arms tightened around her.

"Lass, when we get to Oregon, you can work for me. I'll

keep you safe. I've grown mighty fond of you. You brighten my life, and I enjoy your company. We still have a long ways to go. Now you won't have to fret about your future that whole time." He eased away from her and crawled out of the wagon.

He'd stunned her. His offer was a good one, but she had longed— Well, it wasn't worth thinking about; it would just make her cry. She'd just have to smile if it killed her. More than likely he was interested in one of the single young ladies. They didn't have scars and they weren't full of shame.

She found her ripped dress, and took up a needle and thread. She made quick work of repairing the damage. Then she got dressed and climbed out of the front of the wagon. She didn't want anyone to fuss over her. She'd stay at the next fort. It was really the kindest thing she could do for Heath.

She heard the minster tell everyone they'd be fording the river two times that day. And they'd reach Strawberry Creek. He also said there were trading posts there. Where was the captain? She went back into the wagon, folded the blankets, and put the straw tick on top of a couple trunks.

Taking a deep breath, she then lowered the tailgate and started to climb down. Harrison was there to help her. "I thought maybe you were still sleeping."

"No." She helped herself to a cup of coffee and a few pieces of fried mush and biscuits. Someone already had the beans soaking. By the look of them, they looked to have been soaking since late last night. That would help when they made supper. She didn't make eye contact with anyone. She ate quickly and did what dishes were left to clean. They were staring at her, but she just didn't have it in her to talk. When they finally put the tent in the wagon, she then put in all the crates.

"Luella, I'm sorry I was in the wagon too early for you get

your things. If you need to change or get anything I'll wait here."

"Thank you. I will take you up on that." Luella hopped up and went into the wagon.

Luella was taking a while. Dawn looked for someplace to hide. Just because they didn't want her sliced up didn't mean they wanted her around either.

Luella looked happy when she jumped down. "It seems more and more likely that I'm carrying. I'm overjoyed."

"I'm so happy for you. It's such a special time in a woman's life. Be sure to enjoy it."

"I'd best go talk to Declan before he leaves with the cattle and horses. I'll look for you when I'm walking."

Dawn watched her leave. How she envied Luella. As much as she tried, she couldn't forget the last time she saw her baby. Her heart grew heavy.

Everything was packed up, and she was just about to get inside the wagon when Heath came with the oxen and a drover.

"Dawn, this is Eli. He plans to make a life for himself in Oregon. Aren't you Eli?" The man looked to be about fifty, and his clothes were so stiff with grime she wondered how he moved in them. She found herself standing downwind of him and it wasn't good. She'd smelled plenty worse though.

"It's nice to meet you, Eli. Do you have family traveling with you?"

"No. I never had time or the inclination to marry. Before now, that is." He smiled at Heath.

"It's almost time to leave. Do you know if the Captain was located?" She gazed at Heath.

"Well ma'am, he ate something that didn't agree with him and he had to go dig himself a big hole to sit on. He was there most of the night. It didn't sound like a pretty sight."

"Well yes, I don't think I need any more information. I'm glad he's back."

Eli frowned. "You do know he's married, don't you?"

She didn't acknowledge his insult as she turned away and climbed into the wagon, closed the tailgate and cinched the canvas. Did Eli think she was interested in the captain? The nerve! She sat and laid her forehead against her knees. Did others think that too?

It worried her through one river crossing and then the next one. She stayed in the hot wagon through the nooning. Cora tried to get Dawn to eat but Dawn wasn't hungry. She was still trying to remember talking to the captain and what was said. Had she behaved improperly around him? If that man Eli knew about it, then everyone but her knew it too.

She'd ask Heath about it when they stopped at Strawberry Creek. It was a pretty name.

———

IT WAS a relief to see grass, water, and trees. Heath felt heartened. He'd get Dawn to come out tonight. He'd check out the river first, but maybe he could offer her a swim in the river. He'd have to find out if they were staying an extra day or not. He needed to check all the wheels on both wagons. It got rocky toward the end.

He took their place in the circle and looked into the wagon. She looked so sad and somewhat bewildered. Maybe Luella knew what was` wrong with her. After he climbed down he unyoked the oxen and brought them to be watered. He then rubbed them down with handfuls of grass. Since he'd been doing a lot of the driving lately he hadn't taken care of the livestock, Zander and Declan had that job. He missed being on a horse. Driving cattle wasn't as boring as driving the wagon.

He walked the oxen over to a large area so they could graze with the other animals.

"Heath, wait up!" Eli hurried to him. "If she has her eye on the captain, then why did you think she'd make a good wife for me?"

"I don't think her interest was anything but concern for the person who was leading us to Oregon." Heath shrugged.

"So I still have a chance. She sure is pretty." He scuffed his feet in the dirt. "I know the drawbacks about what happened to her, but I haven't the time or know how to court a woman. I bet they made her work hard. That's what I need, someone who works hard."

"I'm sure your chances are about the same as any. Though you are the first man I've introduced her to."

"Did she say anything about me today?" Eli looked hopeful.

"You know, she was really quiet. I have no idea what it all means."

"I'll be there for supper. See you in a bit."

Declan stopped Heath before he left the area. "I didn't know you and Eli were friendly. He looked as though you were his best friend."

"No you have that unsavory job. I brought him by the wagon this morning to meet Dawn. I got it in my head that she'd have more security if she had a husband. Plus I offered her a job in Oregon. I told her she could live with me, but after I said it I wished I could take it back. It wouldn't be right to have her there with me."

Declan nodded. "I have some good news. Luella is with child." Declan's smile was contagious.

"So soon?"

"Yes, so soon. You're going to be an uncle."

"And you a father. Our lives have changed in the last few months. Congratulations. I'm happy for you both."

"Luella told Dawn about it already. We were going to announce it at supper, but I didn't want it to look like she knew and you didn't. I need to find Zander and tell him. See ya at supper."

Heath walked slowly back to the wagon. That was probably what had Dawn so depressed. It's hard to be happy for someone who is getting what was taken from you. Good thing Eli would be there. Maybe he could take her mind off her problems.

She was busy stirring a pot that hung over the fire. Where was everyone else?

"Do you need any help?" he asked.

"No. I'm just trying to stay busy and out of trouble."

"I hope you made extra. Eli is coming to eat with us."

"As long as I'm up wind of him," she said and smiled. "There's always plenty. I made Cora and Luella go and rest. Oscar the scout stopped by and gave me a rabbit. I impressed him with my quick skinning skills. It feels good to be outside and cooking."

"I'm glad you're not moping around anymore."

"Moping? Is wondering all day what I said or did to make the whole camp think I'm after a married older man moping? Then yes, I was upset and I guess moping. Every time I turn around, I'm accused of some type of misbehavior. I try to be a Godly woman but no one sees that. Maybe if I stepped on the tailgate and started reading really loud from the Bible people would notice. I would never ever think about a married man. I still know right from wrong. I hope wherever you all settle down it's far away from the people talking about me night and day." She took a deep breath. "I have one jar of peaches, and I'm making a pie, so if you'll excuse me." She walked to the tailgate and began gathering ingredients.

He grabbed the tent and set it up for Declan and Luella.

Then he poured himself a cup of coffee after setting up crates around the fire.

Dawn gazed at the tent. "I don't think Luella should be sleeping on the ground. I'm going to insist she sleep in the wagon."

"There's not really enough room for Declan in there too."

"He can sleep under the wagon."

"Where am I supposed to sleep?"

She smiled. "Right outside the tent flap."

"You could offer and see what they say. I'm betting Declan wants to sleep with his wife."

Zander strolled toward them. "I guess we're celebrating tonight, but I'm not allowed to tell anyone."

"Heath invited his friend Eli to eat with us. Are you friends with him too, Zander?"

"I know him. Not all that well. He seems like a good man."

The conversation ended. The others showed up and took a crate. Eli had yet to show up.

"Let's say grace," Dawn suggested. "Declan would you do the honors?"

Declan stood and bowed his head. "Thank You, Lord, for the meal we're about to eat. Thank You for keeping us safe on our journey. I am extremely grateful and thankful that You saw fit to make Luella and me parents. Praise the Lord."

"Amen," the rest chorused.

Declan asked that they do their hugs afterward, when they weren't near the fire. Heath caught his gaze. Most had known about Harrison's first wife. Her dress had caught fire and she had run, only increasing the flames. She had truly suffered before she died.

Cora stood. "Let me help you, Dawn."

"Oh no. You fine women sit back and enjoy yourselves. Everyone has been doing for me, and it's time for me to repay the favor." She dished out the rabbit and bean stew, and when everyone got theirs she passed around the bread. She had just sat down when Eli walked over and sat next to her.

"Yes, I would like some," he said to Dawn.

She didn't look thrilled when she got back up but she gave him food and smiled. They all ate, and Heath watched Eli glancing at Dawn. Twice he moved his crate closer to Dawn's and twice she moved away. She was trying to catch Heath's gaze, but he refused to look at her. He was afraid he'd laugh.

When she sliced the pie and handed Eli his, Heath could see Eli was smitten. His plan to get her married was working.

"Eli, what do you plan to do once you get to Oregon?" Heath asked.

The other man puffed up as he replied. "I'm going to look around for land someone had worked and left. I figure there will be a house built already. I think I'm going to try my hand at farming. I could buy a few chickens, some pigs and cows. I'll probably plant something too."

"Sounds promising." Heath wasn't very convinced that Eli's words had any truth to them. He stood and gathered the empty plates. "I will wash the dishes while Eli and Dawn take a nice walk together."

Eli beamed as he held his arm out to Dawn. She just stood there and then began to walk. Eli fell into step beside her.

"I forgot she doesn't like to be touched. I swear she was shaking right before she started walking," Heath said.

"Since when have you and Eli become friends? Half the time he's useless. You do know he likes to drink?" Zander asked a hint of annoyance in his voice.

"What do you want me to do? If I don't get her married off and out of my life, I'll end up responsible for her and there is no way that is going to happen!" Heath said as he turned to look at Zander.

He hadn't realized that Dawn was standing there behind Zander. Her eyes grew wide and they puddled with tears. She turned and walked away.

Heath closed his eyes. "She heard every word I said. If you could have seen her face… I feel like someone punched me in the gut. Now what should I do?"

"Go after her?"

Heath huffed out a breath in frustration. "You're a lot of help. I best get these dishes done."

"You're not going to go after her? You'll regret it for the rest of your life. I see how you look at her."

"Zander, that's the exact reason I can't go after her. I can't have children with her. People would call them all kinds of names. No child of mine will be born into shame."

"You're a fool, Heath Leary. I'm going to be late for guard duty." Zander stomped off.

WHERE COULD SHE GO? The Shoshone were near. Maybe they'd take her in…or maybe they'd kill her. She got busy and made herself shelter for the night. She'd survive but she'd be alone. Maybe another party would come through and she could act lost or something.

She'd fashioned herself a lean-to to sleep in, and with nothing else to do, she crawled under the leaning branches and cried. She wept from the depths of her soul. How could she not have seen that he held hate in his heart for her? She used to be smarter about life. Now she was just a fool, hoping for a love that would never happen. It might have been better if she'd died when Kills Many threw her off the cliff.

What territory or state was she even in? She didn't know what was ahead, but this area had water and wildlife. She'd build something better to live in when they moved on. There was bound to be snow in the winter here. She'd have time to gather and dry meat. She had little doubt there would be enough carrots, onions, and berries to eat. And there was fish. She quieted, but her soul still felt shredded. A chilled rolled over her and she shivered. Too bad she wasn't wearing something warmer when she had run.

She would have never suspected that Heath felt the way he did. He'd held her on more than one occasion, and how he must have resented it. But no one had asked him. In truth, she had just been put upon him. She'd be better off alone. Her heart couldn't take much more. She didn't know if she could watch both Cora and Luella grow heavy with child while her arms were so very empty.

A noise had her freeze in place and listen. Her name was being called in the distance. She thought she'd gone far enough into the brush. She was sorry for the distress she was likely causing Cora and Luella, but it couldn't be helped. They'd think she got lost or fled. They would move on tomorrow or be left behind.

To be truthful, she had seen Heath as a second chance at love. She only saw what she wanted to see, and the rest she must have made up in her mind. There were mountains not too far. Maybe she could find a trapper who wasn't choosey. That really would be her best bet of surviving, at least for the coming winter. She'd head Northwest. Who knew? She might end up in Canada. Darkness came, and the wolves howled. She wasn't afraid, she had her knife. She'd heard Indians walk by right before sunset. They probably had a camp nearby. She could hunt and make herself warmer clothes. She had learned how to do many things. God had most certainly prepared her for the journey she was to make.

The next morning, her conscience was getting the best of her. People were still calling out her name. Putting her friends through such bother shamed her. It wasn't fair to them. They didn't need more worry. It wouldn't be very Christian of her. Setting things right with God was more important than her hurt feelings.

Dawn crawled out of her lean to and listened. She heard Harrison's voice and walked in that direction. She also heard Heath calling, but she wouldn't bother him again. Harrison took one look at her and his eyes widened.

"We're you attacked? Are you hurt?"

She shook her head. "No, I was a bit lost, but I'm finding my way."

"I know a whole bunch of people who will be happy to see you." He took out his gun and shot it once into the air. "So people will know you've been found."

Harrison put his arm around her shoulder as they walked. The clearing wasn't as far away as she thought. Tears flowed down Cora's face as she ran and hugged Dawn.

"Thank the Lord! Luella!"

"I heard the shot." She stopped and smiled. "You don't know how good it is to see you!" Dawn hugged her and rocked her for a moment.

"I need to go feed Essie. I'll be back to hear what happened." Cora hurried off to her wagon.

Captain London appeared. "That takes a load off my shoulders. I don't think some of the people would move on without you. We leave at first light tomorrow. The women want to wash clothes and take baths. The next part of our journey will be rocky and uphill. The Continental Divide is about a day away. Oh, I want every wagon fixed or maintained and the oxen's feet need to be checked. Some didn't listen to me about putting shoes on the oxen and mules. Fools. Fools never listen to sound advice. You all right, Dawn? You look…well it looks like you had a hard time in the woods."

"I'm fine, really."

"I'm off to go yell at a few fools." The captain walked to the nearest wagon.

Harrison led her to the fire outside his wagon. "Take a seat, and I'll get you some coffee."

"You're a kind man."

"That's why I married him," Cora yelled from inside the wagon.

Harrison handed Dawn the cup of coffee and his face had pinked at Cora's words. Dawn was glad for the reprieve. She was in no hurry to see Heath.

"How are your feet?" Luella asked. "I could check the bandages for you."

"I'd appreciate that. I think they get better every day."

"How long did you walk before you realized you were lost?" Harrison asked.

Declan and Zander both joined them around the fire.

"Not long. I was upset when I ran into the woods. I should have paid more attention. When it started to get dark I made shelter and slept until this morning." She raised her head and her gaze clashed with Heath's.

"You didn't hear us calling for you?" Heath asked.

He was trying to catch her in a lie or make her lie more. She gave him a dismissive look before she turned from him. "I was deep in thought, and of course I was planning what to do if I stayed in these parts."

Everyone nodded and then Luella handed her a plate of food. "What kinds of plans did you come up with?

"I was concerned about the Indians in this area, and I hoped to avoid them. I have no idea what's ahead of us. I finally decided to go into the mountains and see who lived there. Trappers are usually nice men. What I really wanted to do was build my own home. I could live off the land if I had to but I wasn't sure I'd get one done in time."

"I would have panicked," Luella said. "I would have called for Declan over and over and gotten myself caught."

"We're glad you're back," Harrison said. "I'll haul water. I know Cora wants to wash clothes."

Declan stood and kissed Luella on the cheek. "I'll give you a hand."

If things had been different, this would be the time Heath would say he'd help too, since she also had clothes to wash. Everyone else talked and laughed, but she felt so alone.

CHAPTER EIGHT

*D*awn looked as though she'd tussled with a bear all night. Her hair stuck on end in a few places and her face was streaked with dirt. She didn't seem to be harmed. He'd hurt her, and he felt like such a heel.

He didn't even realize he harbored such hated words inside him until they came out. He was tired of everyone thinking Dawn was his responsibility. He was a free man in a free country, and he'd decide who he'd wed or if he'd wed at all. He'd been told what to do his whole life, and for once, he'd like a choice.

She or her children wouldn't bring shame on anyone. He knew that. But he'd said it and she had heard him. Had she planned what to do because she didn't plan to come back? Remorse filled him. He hadn't been a good friend to her.

She finished washing the dishes and started to walk to the other wagon. He got up and hurried to catch her.

"Walk somewhere else please." She quickened her steps.

"I'm sorry for what I said. I didn't know you were there."

"It was for the best," she said in a chilly voice. "Now I know how you really feel. I have depended on you, and that stops now. I can do for myself. I thought I'd ask the women who became widows on this trip if I could travel with them."

No one would agree; he knew it, and from the bleak expression on her face, she knew it too.

"You don't have to go," he said softly. "You cook for me, it's an even trade."

"Heath, I was swirling my head with dreams that have no chance of coming true. I wanted what I had, but what's lost is lost and gone forever. I will never be a wife or mother again. Don't worry, I'll find my place in this world. We'll be passing by traders and there is the fort. I'm hopeful someone will want me to work for them. Someone who sees me and not my shame."

He stopped and allowed her to go on alone. This was his fault. He had led her to believe they could be together eventually. He even offered her a job and acted as though he'd take care of her no matter what. How was he to tell her he hadn't meant a word he said? He just wanted everyone to stop talking about the two of them.

He groaned. Eli stood at the back of the wagon and helped her inside. She deserved better than Eli. Or maybe he was asking her to wash his clothes? Zander and he had better figure out who was going to wash theirs. He doubted Dawn would be so inclined.

Had she been afraid last night? Thankfully she hadn't been taken again. But what about her feet? Would she take care of herself? He'd miss her smiles and how they exchanged glances, the gentle teasing and shared secrets. He'd also miss holding her when she was afraid. And he liked knowing she was asleep right above him.

What had he done? He was looking for husbands for the woman he loved. He drove her away with ugly words. He walked away. He'd make sure the wagon Harrison used was in good shape. Hopefully she wouldn't be in the other wagon when he checked on that one too. His chest tightened and it was hard to breathe. What had he done?

He turned and walked toward Declan. "I don't want to talk about it."

"You don't have to. Zander did your talking for you. I thought you were falling in love. You've been so happy lately, and you always seek her out. I've never seen you as gentle as you are with her. I'm sorry for both of you."

Heath couldn't even look his brother in the eye. "I'm going to go pray on it." He left before Declan could say anything else. He walked down Strawberry Creek and found a place to sit on the bank.

She'd been hit and burned and abused yet he knew he'd hurt her more than that. He'd puzzled her with Eli, but his words hit the target.

Lord, You might as well get it over with and strike me down with lightening. I've never gone out of my way to make someone dislike me before. I took a wounded soul and kicked it hard. I'm the one who is ashamed. She has no shame to bear. She believed it as a possibility and I confirmed it. She's been nothing but kind to me Lord. She clearly doesn't want to talk to me again. Why is it that you don't know how much something means to you until it's gone? I should have been grateful each and every day. In the end my pride got in the way. I thank You for keeping her safe last night. I have no excuse to give her. I don't have a reason to explain to her. I will regret letting her go for the rest of my life. She should stay with the wagon. I'll bed down with the other drovers who don't have a place to sleep. Please forgive me, Father.

He quickly wiped his eyes. Saying sorry and asking for forgiveness were clearly two different things. One was easy enough, and the other was unbelievably scary. That was probably why people said they begged forgiveness. How was he going to do it? If he didn't get it right the first time, there would be no second time.

KEEPING her own council was lonely. She was too embarrassed to tell Cora or Luella why she was upset with Heath, so she kept herself busy in order not to dwell on it. Everything that could carry water was filled. Wagons were once again checked, and some were still were too heavy. Captain London told them that they'd lose plenty of livestock if people didn't take better care.

Declan stood close to the wagon asking them to put as much grass as they could into the back of the wagon. Where they were going, they'd be days without water and food for the oxen. Luella, Cora, and Dawn got busy pulling as much grass from the ground as they could. Not many others were bothering. Hopefully they had lots of grain to feed the animals.

After they collected as much water as they could, Heath and Declan helped gather grass. It was so hard to ignore Heath. She wanted to be done with him but she couldn't help herself, couldn't keep from gazing at him. Their eyes met and held for a moment until she broke it off and turned away. She didn't want him feeling sorry for her.

"Luella, if you'd like to sleep in the wagon I can sleep on the ground. I'm used to sleeping on the ground and I don't want you to catch a chill."

Luella smiled and squeezed Dawn's hand. "You care more about others than yourself. It's sweet, but you need to think about yourself at times. Besides Declan isn't comfortable in the wagon. He likes lots of room."

"I just don't know where I belong," Dawn whispered with a sigh. "My family is dead. I just want to find a place where I honestly belong. Not because they feel sorry for me. I'll never marry, so I just don't know where I belong. I think I'll try to find a place for myself. I don't know what that place may be."

"Don't you go anywhere. You're family to us." Luella hugged her.

Tears filled her eyes, and she struggled to blink them back. She gave her friend a smile. "Thank you."

"We'll be heading out in a few minutes," Harrison announced. It's supposed to be hard going. We're going into the mountains toward the South Pass. I don't want to get stuck behind the heavier wagons. Dawn, I need you to rest for the first part. We'll need everyone to walk about midmorning."

She nodded and swallowed hard when she realized Heath would be the one driving. She climbed into the back without help and grabbed up her Bible.

'I can't have children with her. People would call them all kinds of names. No child of mine will be born into shame.' He didn't know she'd heard that part. She couldn't get his words out of her mind. They had engraved themselves on her heart along with *'If I don't get her married off and out of my life, I'll end up responsible for her, and there is no way that is going to happen.'*

She had never once asked him for anything. Never. She sat near the back of the wagon and watched people walk. She saw a few friendly smiles but by far there were more frowns. She'd heard about a few trading posts run by trappers. If they stopped she would go in and talk to the owner. He might have a few suggestions for her. She couldn't ride into Oregon with Heath.

Why had he told her she had a place in his home? Was he the type of man who told women what he thought they wanted to hear? She'd gotten used to being mistreated. He shouldn't have lied to her. She probably made his skin crawl.

The oxen were working harder and harder trying to pull the wagons to the South Pass. With her bible and shawl, she jumped down from the back. It was time to walk.

Where had her determination gone? What had happened

to her dignity? She felt defenseless and it worried her. She'd had no idea what would happen when Swift Eagle dropped her off. She expected to be treated with kindness and maybe respected for surviving. She stood tall as she walked with her head held high. Taking a few cleansing breaths she made her face expressionless. Perhaps her best bet would be to marry one of the drovers, just not Eli. She'd take a good hard look at the available ones. There was no way she'd end up someone's responsibility.

Her feet hurt but not as much as they had. She could tolerate the pain. She wished she could read and walk at the same time, but it was a rocky road. Three women she had dubbed the widows were behind her. She moved over to let them pass but they didn't.

"We were wondering how you were getting along?" The oldest widow, Mimi Hunt asked.

"I'm fine, thank you." Dawn didn't turn around.

"We wanted to warn you about Eli," Bethenia Blair said. Dawn had always admired Bethenia's thick brown hair.

"What we're trying to say is, he's a drinking, no good lazy bum," Constance Gibney finished.

"Thank you. I appreciate your warning. It's just that I don't have many choices. But I had already ruled Eli out. Plus if there are any you are interested in let me know. I'll take them off my list, not that I have a list. Actually I don't think anyone would want me. I'm thinking about leaving the train and seeing if I can find a place where I could live in peace. I'm not even sure such a place exists."

By now Mimi was walking next to her while Bethenia and Constance were walking right behind them. "I guess we are all widows and we need to watch out for one another. It's hard to know you need a man and the one you love is dead," Bethenia commented.

"We just wanted you to know we understand a bit of what

you are going through, and we've been trying to squash rumors and such. If you need anything we're here. Mimi's husband had built a house and then went back for her. We have a place if you need one." Constance told her.

Dawn's eyes watered. "That is so very kind. Thank you. I've been worrying with each step I take."

"That's why we wanted to walk with you," Mimi told her. "Don't worry once we get to Oregon we won't say a word about you being passed around by the Indians."

Dawn thought her heart would stop. Squashing rumors indeed. They just wanted new rumors to pass on. She needed her mantle to use against the insults. Holding her Bible, she shook her head. "That is very kind of you."

"Dawn, wait up!" Luella called.

"It was a pleasure speaking with each of you," Dawn said.

"We'll talk more later," Mimi promised.

Dawn stopped walking and watched the three women whispering intently. She couldn't trust anyone. She'd had to learn the same lesson time and again but she finally understood it.

"What was walking with those three like?" Luella asked.

"They offered me a place to stay in Oregon and told me if I needed anything I could come to them."

"That's nice of them. I didn't know they could be that nice," Cora said.

"Of course they wouldn't tell anyone in Oregon I'd been passed around by Indians." She barely got the words out without breaking down.

"I'm sorry," Cora said. "You have all of us."

"Actually, I won't be settling near you. Heath offered me a job taking care of his house and told me not to worry about the future. I was stupid enough to take him at his word. I walked back to camp and heard him telling Zander that he needed to marry me off because he didn't want to be responsible for me. I started to run, but I turned back and heard him say he could never have children with me. They would be full of shame."

Luella stopped walking and took Dawn into her arms, hugging her hard. "I didn't know. I'm so sorry. I thought, well never mind what I thought." She let go and took Dawn's hand, holding while they walked.

Dawn saw the worried expression the other two women exchanged. She couldn't bring herself to say anything more. She'd end up on the side of the trail weeping.

"We'll be praying for you," Cora said.

"That's the only thing that will help me. Thank you."

The walk was getting a bit steeper and the mules brayed while the oxen grunted and gave high-pitched moos. Everything was having a hard time.

"If you need someone to take Essie for you Cora, let me know. I know carrying a baby can throw your balance off."

"Cora why don't you walk in front of us. If you fall we're right here," Luella suggested.

Cora stopped and smiled. "You both are too good to me. I'll take you up on your offer for a little while, Dawn. We'll walk behind you."

With the baby in her arms her determination began to come back. She was too young to give up. Maybe she could find work where there is a baby. She had so much faith, yet she couldn't let go of all her worries and give them up to God. Maybe in time.

She didn't need to cloak herself in any mantle when she was with her friends. Yes she did have friends. The feel of Essie against her gave her hope. It wouldn't be easy but she would determine her own future. She was strong in mind, body, heart and faith. So much stronger than many.

How dare Heath treat her like an unwanted pet? One he fed and looked after because that was what was done with a pet. She foolishly lapped up all he had to give. No more; Swift Eagle didn't rescue her to have a life of misery. Every scar, every burn mark were her badges of honor. She had survived while so many hadn't. She'd survived because of her will and her quick mind. She'd survived because God had been with her the whole time and she knew it.

It was hard going but she made it to the top with the help of her friends. She handed Essie back and stood on the flat top alone. South Pass was talked about so much. She could have walked on and never known she'd crossed the Continental Divide. The view was lovely and serene. The rolling hills were welcoming. There looked to be grass further out. She bet they'd stop there for the night.

She looked up to the heavens and decided that her new life started here and now. She knew he was behind her, had sensed him come up. "Too bad it's not steep enough to push me down. But I've been thrown off a cliff before."

He didn't say a word, and she wanted to be the one who walked away not him. She turned and sidestepped to go around him, but he blocked her. Refusing to meet his gaze, she took a deep breath and pretended to be enjoying the view.

"You're nothing but a blackguard, and I'd appreciate it if you'd step aside. I've had a few offers today and I want to think them over." She dared to meet his gaze and the pain he carried puzzled her. Looking away from him she walked away.

They traveled down the pass until they came to Pacific Springs. Everyone was in a festive mood, and by the time supper was done, she heard the first strings of music start. Soon enough she was alone but it was fine.

"Ma'am? Would you like to come dance with me? I heard the whiskey is flowing too." Eli must have combed his hair. It looked better.

"I'm honored to be invited, Eli, bit I'm content to sit here tonight. I'm not much for whiskey." She gave him a smile.

He nodded. His clothes were still filthy but he had tried in his way to look nice. "I understand."

"Have a good evening." She meant it; she did hope he had a good evening.

She thought about going to watch the others dance, but she read her Bible instead. A shadow crossed the pages, and she glanced up. Heath stood there looking as though he was the one alone in the world.

"Not a fan of whiskey either?" she asked.

"Whiskey is fine, but I'd rather dance. You made friends today."

She almost laughed. Her lips twitched. "Yes, I was invited to live with the widows and they couldn't wait to make all the rumors about me go away. It would have been a selfless act except they wanted the real truth from me. I'd rather get my own property and live alone than have to live with them or anyone."

Heath sat down and stared into her eyes. "Anyone, lass? There isn't anyone you'd trust enough to share a roof with?"

"I learned something wonderful. I learned that I am enough. I have the know how to make a life for myself. I'll just need a rifle and I'll have a grand life. I will wake up each morning and greet the Lord and each night I will pray before I sleep. It'll be fine. I see you are sorry for me but I'm done with feeling bad. I never did one thing that was wrong except by force. I've decided to forgive myself for I was powerless. I think I've proven to all that matter that I am a good woman, a shame free woman."

"I'm so—"

"It's not your fault your feel that way Heath. I do blame you for the lie you told me about having a job with you, but it's better to know now." She stood and climbed into the wagon. "Good night, Heath. Don't worry, I won't scratch on the floor ever again. Go dance, Heath. There are plenty of woman who would welcome you." She cinched the canvas closed.

Leaning against the side, she put both hands over her mouth as tears flowed. At least it was done. He would always have a place in her heart.

CHAPTER NINE

*T*he next day they continued on and stopped at a place called the Parting of the Ways. There was a big decision to make. Taking the Sublette Cutoff was shorter, but it was waterless. The other way was longer, but they stopped at Fort Bridger to resupply.

Heath had a meeting that morning with Harrison, and Harrison wanted to take the longer path. It was easier on the livestock. Heath was glad; he had no desire to travel through one hundred miles of sand. It seemed too big of a chance since there wasn't water.

Heath shook his head as Tom Simps led a motley crew into the desert, including Eddie and Chuck Klass. He watched as Cora hugged her friend Sally Waverly. Rod Waverley was convinced they were going the better way.

He was surprised by the number of people who were willing to take a chance on Sublette Cutoff. They would all meet again at the Bear River. He kept turning around making sure that Dawn was going their way. A while later, he noticed she was limping. He pulled off and waited for her. At first she frowned at him, but he caught relief on her face as she climbed onto the wagon. She sat as far away from him as she could on the bench.

He hoped they would talk but she didn't glance his way. He didn't know what to say or do.

"The hunters have returned. It looks like they got enough food for all of us."

She looked around and grinned. "They got a bear. I haven't had bear in a long while. Supper will be something to look forward to."

"I confess I haven't had bear before."

"I'd had it on occasion when Lincoln would go hunting. There was much meat to be had, and of course the bear skin made a good rug. If I had known how to cure the skin we could have used them as blankets. It's hard work scraping and scarping the skin. But I now know how. Of course a bear is nothing to fool with. They are hard to kill."

"Was the house you and your husband had nice?"

She nodded. "It ended up much bigger than I thought it would. Lincoln liked to surprise me that way. It was made of logs, and there were four bedrooms. I guess he expected a big family." She blushed. "He could be stubborn, and his word was final, but I figured I could cure him of that eventually. He did listen to my opinion and I liked that. He was a good father. How he loved Patricia, it was heartwarming to watch the two of them together. I used to wonder what our life would have been like if the Lakota never came. But I learned that dreaming about things that couldn't be only hurt and made my heart harder to heal."

"I'm so sorry about what happened to your family. I am proud of the way you survived. I can't imagine coming out of there with my life. Maybe at the fort you can contact whoever you need to. I bet they'd like to know you're alive."

"I meant it when I said there was no one. My parents and his both died of small pox. We lost many in our settlement, but it didn't spread any further. It was a hard time, but Lincoln and I saw each other through it. What do you suppose other woman who escaped have done? Did their community embrace her when she returned? I would have thought yes, but from the attitudes of many I've seen, I don't think it the case. If a woman was taken by outlaws and she escaped but she'd endured many of the same things, do you think people would turn their backs on her?"

"Probably not. I wish I could have made things easier for you." He sighed.

"I learned a lot from you. I'm wiser for it."

She turned from him and watched the land they passed.

When they did stop, she made supper and smiled at everyone. She had them fooled, but he could see her pain. After the chores were all done, he heated water and found strips of cloth to use. Then he sat on the crate next to her and put her foot on his thigh. Her eyes widened but she didn't pull away.

He cleaned her foot. Her feet were still full of scabs and open wounds. When he was done, she nodded at him.

"Thank you. They feel better than they did. The moccasins help. I bet you have plenty of other things you'd rather be doing, though, and I'm fine here alone."

"Maybe I enjoy your company," he said.

She shook her head and glanced away. "Please don't. It hurts too much. I'm not your responsibility. I lost control of my feelings for a while but I've hardened my heart. I'm not sure if I can take being hurt like that again. I'm going to bed."

"It's early."

"I know. I think I'll light the candle lantern and read for a bit. Good night."

She was getting mighty quick at getting into the wagon. He should have said he was sorry and begged her forgiveness. Maybe she's right. He didn't know anything about relationships. How was he going to convince Dawn he didn't mean the things he said. He didn't want Zander to start making comments about her. He wasn't the nicest at times.

He stood and waited until the light flickered inside the wagon. "Dawn, I need my bedroll."

He heard rustling, and the canvas opened. She held his bedding out to him. "I didn't think that the rest of you might need something."

He took the bedroll. She was so utterly beautiful with her hair unbound. He wanted to touch it, but he knew better. He smiled his thanks, and when he turned around, he found Patty Mince sitting at the fire. She was always trying to get him alone but he thought he'd let her down gently enough, Yet, here she was again.

"Good evening, Heath." She battered her eyelashes at him.

"Does your father know where you are?"

"I'm old enough. Besides, I thought you had feelings for the Indian woman. Since now I know you can't stand her, here I am."

"You must have heard wrong." He sat on a crate across the fire from her. "Patty, you're a bit young for me. I know we talked about it before."

"I'm fifteen now. I just had a birthday. I'm old enough. Besides I think we would get on just fine plus I told my father we were getting married."

Before Patty had the word marriage out, Dawn was dressed and out of the wagon.

"I didn't realize you had company, Heath." She sat on a crate next to him.

"Dawn, this is Patty."

"It's nice to meet you," Dawn said and then smiled. "Where is that young man you usually spend your evenings with? Bobby I think is his name."

Patty narrowed her eyes as she stared at Dawn. "He's just

a boy. He wouldn't be able to take care of a wife and a family. Plus his parents need him to help work the new land. Women are more mature than boys, don't you agree?"

"I don't know. I guess it depends. I was married at sixteen, but Lincoln had been building our house for a year before he asked me to marry him. He was eighteen, and I never felt we were too young."

"How old are you know? You look like you're about thirty years old. Your skin isn't soft or dewy like a young woman."

"I'm almost twenty but I feel much older. I'm sure I lost that dewy look the day my husband and baby were killed." She angled her head and stared openly at Patty. "I didn't know you and Heath were so close."

Patty nodded. "We have been from the first night on the trail. At least until you came and took up his time."

Dawn turned and met Heath's eyes. "Heath, you could have had someone else take care of me. You never once mentioned you had a young lady friend."

He didn't know what to say. Somehow, Patty was trying to rope him into marriage.

"Does your father know you're to have a child?"

Patty gasped and Heath stared at Dawn. So that was the reason Patty was here. He had never even held hands with the child. How did Dawn know Patty was expecting?

"Patty, you need to tell your father the truth," Heath said, trying to sound firm.

"I want to be able to tell him we're getting married first. Of course I don't know where you'd live, Dawn." She all but smirked.

"Dawn is here at the invitation of the Walshes. I don't own a thing. I share the space under the wagon with Zander. I work for wages of which I'm saving every penny. You do know how to work a ranch, don't you? Milk cows, clean out the horse stalls, wash the clothes, cook the meals, help with the butchering of the pigs each fall?" Heath tried to be as serious as possible. If she named him the father, he'd have to marry her. He glanced at Dawn. There was only one woman he loved, and he'd made such a muddle of things but he wasn't ready to give up.

"I'm sure we can hire someone. I'll have the baby to take care of."

"What about the father? Doesn't he have a right to know? It is his child too."

"Heath I know this is a shock. I'll give you a day to mull it over before my father comes after you with a shotgun. We will be married." She stood and with a toss of her head, she turned and walked toward her wagon.

"I never—"

Dawn reached over and took his hand. "I know you didn't. She's determined, and I'm sorry but I think you'll have to marry her."

"It's not her I love." He stared into her blue eyes for a few long minutes. Then he nodded, confident Dawn loved him. "You'd best get some sleep." He smiled at her. He stood and lifted her into the wagon. "Good night, lass. Thank you for coming to my rescue."

She gave him the sweetest smile he'd gotten from her in weeks. His heart contracted. What if it was the last smile she ever gave him? He'd fight Patti with everything he had but in the end it was usually the girl with child who was believed.

It wasn't fair. He really thought there would be a chance for him and Dawn. He figured he's have months yet to convince her that he loved her. He'd caused her such pain and he never meant to. Would he wake up to a shotgun in his face with Mr. Mince at the other end of it? He shook his head. He really wouldn't be able to hire any help at first but Patti didn't take it as truth. It was a doomed marriage he wished he could run from.

"Dawn, wake up!" Luella's urgent voice roused her.

Dawn's heart pounded with fear. "What?"

"Patty Mince's Pa is out for blood. We need you to marry Heath and now."

Dawn sat up and watched as Luella went through her trunk and started pulling things out. She took out one dress and her eyes lit up.

"Did you make this? It's beautiful, and the blue matches your eyes. Well, come on I know you want to rescue him, don't you?"

Dawn quickly got up and started washing with the warm water in the basin Luella must have brought in. She got dressed while Luella tried to keep up with her and brush her hair.

"You look lovely. Cora and I decided we'd both stand up for you. If you'll have us."

Dawn laughed. "Good. Has Mr. Mince gotten the shot gun yet?"

"No, but we expect him back with one any time."

Dawn went to the back of the wagon and there waiting for her was Heath. He looked freshly shaved and he had a clean new shirt on. He looked so handsome.

"You're beautiful." He held his arms up and grasped her around the waist and set her down.

They didn't get to speak to one another. Reverend Paul and his wife Della were there, and the next thing she knew they were married. She glanced around and discovered even Captain London was there. Heath barely kissed her, and she was just as glad. She started to shake when he got closer. Hopefully, with time she'd be able to allow him to kiss her. She did hold his hand and didn't object when he laced his fingers through hers.

It all happened so fast, she almost forgot about Patty until Mr. Mince stood in front of them with his rifle. He pointed it at them and Heath immediately put her behind him.

"I suggest you have a conversation with Bobby. I never even looked at Patty. She's a nice kid, but that's all it is. I bet Bobby's parents have no idea where he's been most nights."

"Reverend, come with me," Mr. Mince said, his mouth forming a grim line as he seemed to acknowledge the likely truth of Heath's words. "You will be performing another marriage this day."

Captain London muttered that it best be a quick wedding as they needed to get going.

After a few hugs, she was left alone with Heath. The words he said to Zander came back to her. "I'll go change." She turned from him and climbed into the wagon before he was close enough to help her.

Dismay washed over her. What had she done? She'd tied herself to a man who thought she brought shame with her. Marriage wasn't easy, and she couldn't help but worry. She put on her calico dress and stepped down out of the wagon.

Breakfast was made and ready for her to eat. Most of the dishes were washed. Heath sat by the fire drinking coffee. He didn't look particularly upset.

"Come on Mrs. Leary, let's have breakfast together on this grand day."

She took her plate and coffee and sat next to him. "I know you didn't want to get married, Heath, and I'm sorry it was me you ended up with." She held up her hand to stop him from talking. "You know I don't know if I could ever be a proper wife to you and you deserve better than me. I'm battered and scarred. I'm not pretty with unblemished skin. I married you to help a friend. I have no illusions it's anything else. We do well as friends, so maybe we can be friends again or you could leave me at the Fort. I'd never think less of you if you did."

"Wagons ho!" came Captain London's call.

She jumped up and began to pack the last few things into the wagon. Then she scrambled on the bench while Heath yoked the oxen.

She couldn't help but compare this wedding to the one she'd had with Lincoln. There had been so much happiness she thought she'd burst from it. They'd all danced until the wee hours of the morning. Everything had been lovely. But now...

Swallowing hard, she put a smile on to face the day.

Heath climbed up and they were off, getting into line. It would probably be a long day of travel. They were days away from the fort, and she needed to make a huge decision. She could be brave and give Heath his freedom while she stayed at the fort. She'd find her way. She knew she would.

"That was quite the morning," he said.

"Yes, I've never had Luella wake me before. She rummaged through my trunk and found my dress."

It's a fine dress. Did you make it?"

"Yes, it's one I worked on after I made the shirts for you and useful dresses for me. I don't know why I made it actually. I can't hide who I am. I wish you had another option. Marrying me must have been hard." She didn't want to hear pretty words from him. She just wanted to speak the plain truth.

He didn't say anything for a while and then in a great baritone voice he sang

Of all the money e'er I spent,
I spent it in good company.
And all the harm I've ever done,
Alas! it was to none but me.
And all I've done for want of wit

To mem'ry now I can't recall
So fill to me the parting glass
Good night and joy be with you all.
Oh, all the comrades e'er I had,
They're sorry for my going away,
And all the sweethearts e'er I had,
They'd wish me one more day to stay,
But since it falls unto my lot,
That I should rise and you should not,
I gently rise and softly call,
Good night and joy be with you all.
If I had money enough to spend,
And leisure time to sit awhile,
There is a fair maid in this town,
That sorely has my heart beguiled.
Her rosy cheeks and ruby lips,
I own she has my heart in thrall,
Then fill to me the parting glass,
Good night and joy be with you all.

"That was beautiful, you have a nice voice."

"It's called The Parting Glass, and though there is no fair maid I do have a fair lass who has my heart in thrall. So you see it was no hardship marrying you. I've loved you for a while now. I'm a stubborn man, but my eyes have been opened. I cannot be without you. I've made many mistakes, and I ask your forgiveness. If we never have children, we'll have each other. I was glad we married. I was afraid you were going to leave, and that I could not live with. And you are beautiful, very beautiful. The Lord blessed me today, and I'm so very grateful. I would like to sleep next to you, though. We can get our own wagon at the fort. We'll be there in a few days."

"Are you sure? I don't want to be someone you married because you felt sorry for me. I have found that I am strong and capable. I'd like you to come to services with me. They only last ten minutes at the most. God has kept me safe in the palm of his hand, and just because I'm happy I shouldn't forget all the love he has bestowed on us both."

"Yes, I will attend services. I have much to thank God for. You haven't said anything about how you feel about me." He almost looked worried.

She smiled. "You mean the world to me. My soul is no longer bruised, and my heart is no longer broken. I look at you, and I see a future that is long and loving. I love you, Heath Leary. It's nice to finally know where I stand with you. I want children so I will work hard to get over my fear. You'll have to be patient."

"I can do that. Just knowing you love me makes me feel stronger and a better man. I swear I didn't mean what I said. I'm proud to have you as my wife, and I'll welcome any children we have. I don't want you just as a wife. I want you as a partner in our new adventures together. I'm ashamed of what I said and the words weren't true. I never loved a woman before. I liked everything about you and I couldn't wait to catch a glimpse of you or talk to you. Taking care of your feet brought me closer to you. Holding you in my arms was heaven. You scared me though. Despite needing me you were remarkably able to do for yourself. I was afraid you'd decide you didn't need me or want me. My heart broke when I left the land where I was born. Actually it broke well before that with each starved face I saw. You made my heart whole again and it scared me."

She put her hand on his arm. "God gave me back my ability to believe in wishes again. I wished for you, for us and then decided I wasn't in a position to wish. God gave me the one thing I wished for and that was you. I will be a good wife to you, Heath. I hope we have children sooner than later but..."

"We have a lot of time my love. We'll have a fine life in Oregon." He took his eyes off the trail and kissed her. Looking up he corrected the oxen and got back on the trail. "I love you."

"I love you too."

NEXT UP WILL BE Zander's turn. He can be not so nice at times. Is there a woman out there that can help him change? Word of mouth really made this series take off and I so appreciate you!

Right now I'm toying with the idea of writing a Christmas book with these characters. One that is in the future, so we can see how our favorite characters' lives turn out. Right now I want to know if Dawn and Heath ever have children. If you have a question about a character let me know and I'll see if I can work it into the story.

THE END

I'm so pleased you chose to read Dawn's Destiny, and it's my sincere hope that you enjoyed the story. I would appreciate if you'd consider posting a review. This can help an author tremendously in obtaining a readership. My many thanks. ~ Kathleen

ABOUT THE AUTHOR

Sexy Cowboys and the Women Who Love Them...
Finalist in the 2012 and 2015 RONE Awards.
Top Pick, Five Star Series from the Romance Review.
Kathleen Ball writes contemporary and historical western
romance with great emotion and
memorable characters. Her books are award winners and
have appeared on best sellers lists including: Amazon's Best
Seller's List, All Romance Ebooks, Bookstrand, Desert
Breeze Publishing and Secret Cravings Publishing Best
Sellers list. She is the recipient of eight Editor's Choice
Awards, and The Readers' Choice Award for Ryelee's
Cowboy.
Winner of the Lear diamond award Best Historical Novel-
Cinders' Bride
There's something about a cowboy

    f facebook.com/kathleenballwesternromance
    y twitter.com/kballauthor
    O instagram.com/author_kathleenball

OTHER BOOKS BY KATHLEEN

Lasso Spring Series

Callie's Heart

Lone Star Joy

Stetson's Storm

Dawson Ranch Series

Texas Haven

Ryelee's Cowboy

Cowboy Season Series

Summer's Desire

Autumn's Hope

Winter's Embrace

Spring's Delight

Mail Order Brides of Texas

Cinder's Bride

Keegan's Bride

Shane's Bride

Tramp's Bride

Poor Boy's Christmas

Oregon Trail Dreamin'

We've Only Just Begun

A Lifetime to Share

A Love Worth Searching For

So Many Roads to Choose

The Settlers
Greg

Juan

Scarlett

Mail Order Brides of Spring Water
Tattered Hearts

Shattered Trust

Glory's Groom

Battered Soul

Romance on the Oregon Trail
Cora's Courage

Luella's Longing

Dawn's Destiny

Terra's Trial

Candle Glow and Mistletoe

The Kabvanagh Brothers
Teagan: Cowboy Strong

Quinn: Cowboy Risk

Brogan: Cowboy Pride

Sullivan: Cowboy Protector

Donnell: Cowboy Scrutiny

Murphy: Cowboy Deceived

Fitzpatrick: Cowboy Reluctant

Angus: Cowboy Bewildered

The Greatest Gift